Andrew

04. 08. 07

Feelgood

By Simon Ford

BookBay

BookBay
Crediton EX17 5HQ

Published by BookBay

Copyright © Simon Ford 2006

Simon Ford asserts the moral right to
be identified as the author of this work.

ISBN: 0-9554547-0-0

ISBN: 978-0-9554547-0-7

FEELGOOD

1.

Feelgood is addictive. It commands the brain. Free will is nothing but a servant to its cravings. Feelgood creates dependence. Its rush is the best of all . Even good people do bad things at its mercy.

He stepped through a small doorway cut low into a massive pair of prison gates. The grim spring light, the cars passing on the street below, the warm gust of human endeavour- they were all enchanting. He set off along the pavement, heading west across the city. No home, no job, no faith. Just his passport and his savings. In his heart joy. The nowness of things complete, affirmed with every step.

There were a few market stalls set up along the High Street pavement. Little shops sheltering under scaffold sections and taut plastic roofing sheets. The same goods and the same faces. Cheap tools, batteries, vacuum cleaner bags, dried flowers. The end stall was still as before. A tall man stooped amidst thick Parkas on coat hangers, piles of soiled khaki trousers and scuffed boots. He showed his list and the stallholder smiled faintly and reached towards the back of a van laden with more clothing. Lurking in the corner, he tried on the things that were handed to him, and within half an hour he had what he needed. All of it showing the distress of the parade ground or the battlefield. Perhaps someone had killed or been killed in these clothes. They haggled a while over the price. When he offered his old outfit in part exchange the stallholder weakened. Pity or solidarity, he couldn't tell.

He had black lace-up boots in fair condition, with some tread left and a waterproof lining. Dark green cotton trousers with large side pockets. Silk thermals, Norwegian army shirt with zip-up high collar. Windproof fleece and waterproof jacket. A woollen beret and a canvas rucksack. Inside it were overtrousers, a bivi bag and a set of cooking utensils. Just as he was leaving there was a touch on his arm and he was handed a bowie-knife in a leather sheath. No words, just a little nod and that faint smile.

He picked up some candles, a head torch and a pack of disposable lighters from a nearby stall and headed west. This time a little warily. His feet felt strange in the boots,whilst the trousers were damp and stuck to his knees. He took deep breaths of city air through his nostrils, euphoria swirling. He wanted to hold the moment, so free yet full of necessity. Food, shelter, movement, they were all down to him once again. Not idle concerns but a pressing need.

He glanced at the list and crossed over the street towards an electrical goods store. He picked out a little walkman radio, not much bigger than a cigarette packet with lightweight headphones that folded away. Only £40 left. He turned off the High Street into Cathedral Square, for the pleasure of it. All quiet still, too early for the buskers and the tourists. A few couples rubbed together on benches. He sat amongst them and stared openly. No-one seemed to notice, or mind. For every moment that he had lain looking at a white-washed wall, there might have been someone here. In love, maybe in despair.

Across the Green by a low wall sat a group of cider drinkers. Matted hair, pierced bodies, mongrel dogs asleep or sniffing about. A few faces looked up as he passed, assessing him with mild curiosity. He stood on the steps to gaze at the great Oriel window and the ornate stone carvings. He had stood here before once, but as the memory came he strangled it and turned back towards the High Street.

The road soon narrowed and began to slope steeply down to the river, leaving the big shops and chainstores behind. He bought a catapult, the type with a brace for the forearm, and some steel ammo. He selected a few paperbacks from the secondhand bookshop, and then he crossed over the river on a new footbridge down by the weir. The floodplain on the far side was a large park, dotted with football pitches and play areas. Most popular by far was a fenced off yard with concrete humps and dips where young boys on skateboards and small-wheeled bikes performed for one another. Beyond the plain the land rose steeply up towards the hills. He was looking for the start of a small lane that headed west through a wooded valley. Or used to. For a while he felt disorientated. The trees had gone, and terraced into the hillside were hundreds of small homes looking back across the river to the city. Bungalows, flats, detached houses with little gardens, all served by a myriad of new access roads. A supermarket had been built at the foot of the hill. He went in to ask the way, and came out with two large bags of rice and porridge oats, a bottle of olive oil, and some vegetables.

Now his rucksack felt like a true burden. The straps dug into his collar bones. He was glad of the discomfort. Glad of the burning in his calves and the sweat on his forehead as he headed uphill through the neat rows of houses and parked cars. West.

2.

He reached the chapel at dusk. Travelling along empty country lanes between high hedges. The odd farm, a long view south once through a gateway down to the estuary and the sea. Another view north over a wide fertile plain.

The chapel was set back from the road in a little fenced paddock, surrounded on three sides by massive oak trees. No village, not even a hamlet. Just one old farmhouse a way off, then woods and fields down into the distance. Where had all the people lived who once came to worship here? Their houses of cob and thatch had dissolved back into the earth. It was too remote up here in the hills, on the road to nowhere.

He followed a little gravel track around to the porch on the south side. The door was unlocked. Inside a few simple pews, a plain altar, no stained glass. Framed on the wall a bizarre account of how some worshippers had been killed when their carriage horses bolted on the way back to the City.

He gathered a little deadwood from around the oaks and together with the fir cones he had found on the road he made a fire. So many nights he had spent dreaming of this. Squatting by a fire, arranging a few stones to support a pan and boiling a little rice. Later he played with the radio to see what he could pick up. When he climbed into his bivi bag under the lee of the roof, he knew he was entirely content. Without worry. Without fear.

How strange that first night of freedom, rolled up against the Chapel wall. The stillness of it. His brain ought to have been troubled. The slammed doors, the keys, the shouting were missing. Instead, he let go the past and drifted with the country night. Everything in him anticipated the dawn. And when at last it came and the chorus of birdsong began, the pleasure of it overwhelmed him. He gave way to tears and the certainty that never would he have listened so acutely had it not been missing for so long. Those many different songs of welcome and reassurance.

After a while he was aware that he had company. On the dry earth between the roots of an oak lay a tortoiseshell cat. It had assumed a big cat pose, with legs splayed out to the side and tail gently tapping. It was observing him, so cool and fearless. He had the feeling he was being assessed for his ability to survive in the wild.

He set off again mid-morning. The tarmac road ended just beyond the farm entrance, giving way to an ancient green lane with tall earth banks on either side. Turning a corner, he stopped suddenly and rested the rucksack on the ground. Ahead was an open view across the valley. And on the other side his destination. The excitement in him was childlike. He wanted to dance. Instead he kept quite still, smiling and looking across at his new home. He wasn't disappointed. The clump was just as he remembered it, a thickly wooded mop on top of a hill, and gently sloping cheeks of red earth sown with wheat, barley, and

6

maize. Such fertile land. The farms had been built down in the valley below. The only building on the hill was an old Georgian house. He couldn't see from this side, but he remembered it and knew it would be there, half-hidden by trees on the south side looking across to the Moor.

He took up the rucksack and set off again down the hill. There was a river at the bottom, and only a ford for a crossing. The water came in over the top of his boots and he squelched into the village, rejoining the tarmac road. The old Post Office had become a Post Office Stores, and he went in to buy some milk.

'On your holidays are you?' The woman behind the counter masked her curiosity behind a cheery smile.

'Sort of. I hope to stay around for a bit, so I'll maybe be in again.'

He left wondering how his voice had sounded. Surly perhaps, or just embarrassed. He was still awkward, and a little self-conscious around others. It was hard to believe that they couldn't see his recent past, made up on his face.

He found the turn-off up the hill. A narrow lane that began steeply, then levelled off a little, snaking its way through fields to the wooded summit. It was used by tractors, and the odd car going to the Georgian house. No-one overtook him as he made his way up, weighed down by his pack. The magic of his journey was diminishing, the nearer he came to his destination.

3.

The gateway was thoroughly overgrown, which was encouraging. He eased his way in carefully, trying not to disturb things too much until he was out of sight of the road. Then he took out the bowie-knife and slashed his way forward along what had once been a cart track between tall ash and oak trees. It curved first to the right, then to the left and suddenly he was free of the brambles and branches and what he saw felled him to his knees.

7

He reached forwards for support and calmed himself to look again.

He was at the entrance to an ancient quarry. The rock face was at least 30ft high and mostly sheer, formed in the shape of a horseshoe with himself at the opening. From where he was you could either walk down a slope into the centre, or scramble up some rocks to the side and find your way around the top of the cliff.

Since the quarrymen had left, the trees had taken over. There was a magnificent canopy above him, forming a domed roof to the old workings. Oak, ash and beech grew right up to the rim of the crater and stretched their arms protectively over it. Mingled in amongst them were larch and Scots pine, eye-catching at this time when the broad leaves were still only in bud. Light filtered through and warmed the rockface, but not enough to let trees grow on the quarry floor. It was open, and those saplings which did take root were nibbled back with the grass by rabbits and deer. In the far corner a spring rose near the foot of the rockface, and trapped by the slope the water formed a little pond before filtering down through the layers beneath.

It was a perfect amphitheatre, coproduced by nature and man, to form a stage for his imaginings. Sheltered from the world and its weather, he knew that here he might rest and heal. He stood up, and leaving the rucksack he walked over to the right hand rockface, which looked south and kept warmest and brightest. In the middle at ground level was a small cave, large enough for two people to lie down in, and by it the remains of a wooden door which had once been fashioned to cover the entrance. In front of the cave was a flat, grassy terrace, quite dry, and ideal for sitting out and cooking. It was better even than he had remembered it. A memory which had sustained him through the sag of seven years.

He was unprepared for the light inside the quarry. The rock composed an igneous, rich, red sandstone, in places smooth and shiny, elsewhere bubbled in texture. The sun that found its way through the canopy was both absorbed and reflected by the sandstone, forming a dappled, ruddy gloaming.

He needed to get busy or he felt that he would just stand there grinning like a fool until nighttime. He set about gathering rocks to build himself a hearth for his new home. Deadwood was plentiful all about, but he needed to collect enough to maintain a fire alight constantly. That way he could keep the embers hot and minimise the danger of starting wet and cold fires. There was little possibility that the smoke would hang together long enough to give away his position, but he preferred not to leave it to chance. Once the rucksack was unloaded it served well as a carrier for his journeys back and forth, foraging for firewood, and dry bedding for the cave. There were ferns aplenty, and it was too early in the year to worry about ticks hiding on the fronds.

By evening he had dragged home a good stack of logs and dead branches for the fire, and the cave floor was cushioned with dry leaves and vegetation. He climbed in rearwards to try it out, lying on his back with his feet by the entrance and his head propped against a pile of clothes and provisions deep inside. He could look out to the hearth, and beyond to the opposite wall of rock. He was so happy to swap his cell bunk for this tiny den all to himself. He thought how many of his fellow inmates would be reluctant to live as he intended .

Only one thing was missing. Fire. The first flame was to him as important as any in his life. He had kept the ceremony until he felt prepared and at ease. Sitting cross-legged on the grass behind his circle of chosen stones, he flicked a lighter to set fire to some dry leaves and fir cones. The flames were his and he fed them generously.

The motion of feeding the fire took him back. He saw himself as he had been as a boy, lodged in the crook of a cherry tree and reaching out his arms rhythmically to pick the ripe fruit and carry it to his mouth. With another leap backwards he saw himself as one of his primitive ancestors, making fire and gathering berries and nuts. His brain held memory from other lifetimes.

4.

He didn't leave the quarry for three days. Morning and evening he took up the radio and searched for music or current affairs, but he had no stamina for news and after a while he would put it away again. He set about improving his terrace with an awning made of ash poles lashed together with stripped bark and thatched with ferns. This kept the worst of the rain out of the cave and away from the log store.

His greatest pleasure was observing and listening. His home was a watching loft, and from it he could follow the life of the wood which surrounded him. At dawn a chorus of pent up courtship washed away his sleep and fixed upon him a mood of acceptance and contentment which lasted the whole day. Across on the other side of the quarry he had fashioned a sort of bird table where he would leave a few scraps and some porridge oats. At first the shock of his coming was so great that nothing came to the quarry floor, but by the third day the woodland creatures were already adapting to his presence. Some blue tits had visited the table, he had seen rabbits grazing cautiously a way off in the evening, and he had once been electrified to hear the outrage of the roe deer when they sensed his intrusion.

On the fourth morning he had no milk for his porridge. He had kept the container cool by submerging it in the pond. Water was a poor substitute in porridge and he resolved to go down to the Post Office and buy a few provisions with the last of his money.

The woman there smiled at him in recognition, asking politely if he was enjoying his stay and all the while her eyes asked a good many questions besides. He bought milk, a pot of local honey and some fresh bread, which was delivered daily to the shop.

As he left, a card in the window caught his attention. A campsite owner was looking for part time help for the new season. Someone to clean and to mow the grass. He had only a few pounds left in his pocket, and this might be work paid in cash without too many questions asked. He knew the campsite, which was the other side of the village on an ancient water meadow. It was the reason he was here now. As a boy, his family had come for the summer holidays. He and his brother had first stumbled across the quarry on a daring, unsanctioned expedition of their own one afternoon, and they had been harshly rewarded for such boldness. Their distraught parents were on the point of calling the police from the village phonebox.

He smiled at the memory and resolved to go on there straightaway and apply for the job. As he walked, more and more his doubts walked alongside. He had no address, no references, no way to account for his recent past, excepting the truth, and he was, he realised with sudden conscience, grubby and unshaven. What kept him on his course was the recollection he had of the campsite owner. Yet it might so easily have changed hands in the intervening thirty years.

He came to the entrance and looked in over the gate. His first impression was that things were so much smaller than before. Chasing around and around on his first bike, the place had once seemed the size of a prairie. A tarmac drive led to the wooden service block, built in the middle of the field beneath the branches of an oak tree. It housed rubbish bins, loos, sinks, showers and an office. All around, the field was flat and smooth as a lawn, the grass already closely mown. No marked out pitches or plug in mains points. Guests just parked up to suit themselves.

An old man came out of the office. He walked keenly forward, disguising a limp and a stooped back. They met over the gate.
    'You keep the old place just as neat and tidy as ever, then.'
The owner studied him closely for a few moments before he replied.
    'I can't stand to see it let go. Trouble is, these days what with my knee and all, I'm only good for sitting in the office. The place never makes any money and they say I should pack it in, but I couldn't bear to turn away the ones been coming here year after year. Besides, what on earth would I do with myself all day, under the wife's feet, if I couldn't get away down here?'

The encouragement was obvious. It was taken up.

'I saw your card in the window up at the Post Office. I've happy memories of staying here, it must be thirty years ago now. I could do with the money if you'd take me on. Trouble is, I've no name and no past, if you understand me. No address either.'

The old man's eyes held his in a duel of generous and worldly amusement. At last he replied.

'Don't care who you are or where you spring from as long as you're honest and reliable. Start the day after tomorrow if that suits you. Two or three hours in the morning, every other day. You can use the showers after work. Looks like you could do with a wash, now and then.'

The two men shook hands over the gate. The old man limped back towards his office, and the other headed home up the hill.

5.

Life is a device with diminishing returns. In prison he had found time enough to learn about his world. The Big Bang won't explode outwards forever. Expansion gives way to contraction. Then comes the Degenerate Age. Matter will decompose.

He dreamt that he recognised the exact moment in his own life when the horizon ceased to recede and decay set in.

He woke in fear. The first fear since his release. For a while, his brain broadbanded trying to process information and memory at frantic speed . Then he heard it again, clearly. A hunting horn. Coming from somewhere down by the river. Followed by the cry of a few hounds, but with little conviction. He guessed they were hunting mink along the riverbed, and imagined the followers oblivious to the wet and cold on their purposed wadings.

The fear lingered and launched him from the cave. He grabbed at his boots. His subconscious had leapt with sly agility from one hunt to another. A manhunt. Now he understood his fear and welcomed its firebrand searing the stillness of his idyll. It was time to face the possibility. They might come for him. They had tried to get at him the first year inside. He knew there had been a contract out. Nothing since, but they would wait, steadfast in the desire for revenge, until he was released. Now it would be cheaper and easier to administer their justice.

He sat reviving the fire to cook breakfast and his sang-froid returned. He was calmed by his surroundings, reassured by his wild friends. They would sound the alarm if anyone tried to penetrate the quarry.

Yes, his release would be known about. But no-one could have followed him along the lanes from the city and stayed unseen. Besides, he had been an easy target on his journey, so why wait. He had kept the destination his secret and he was certain they could'nt yet know his whereabouts. That had been the reason to avoid a release under licence, and an enforced parole. Instead he had seen to it that he served out his full sentence. He had needed to disappear without trace, at least to begin with, to leave them no scent.

It was his morning at the campsite. On his trips up and down the hill his stride had become impatient. The rhythm and pace of walking did not suit him. Yet only a few months ago he would have settled for a lifetime's walking in exchange for his freedom. The shadow of diminution had rejoined him.

There were only a few campers this early in the season. They stood around the service block, their voices a little too loud and their faces animated by the drama of the morning. To be woken by the energy and assault of the hunt, to peer out at the medley of hounds, horn and huntsmen, this was an extraordinary event. They swirled childlike in its slipstream.

He set about his tasks. Cleaning sinks, loos and showers. Scrubbing, sponging and wiping the surfaces. Mopping the screed floor last of all. Chores he knew well from his early years in prison. Once the block was clean, he went over to the little shed sheltered in a corner beneath the hedge. He unlocked the doors and checked over the mower for grease, oil and fuel. Then he pulled the ancient engine into life, and set off to mow his broad stripes, perched above a little trailed roller.

At midday in the office, the old man thanked him for his work and handed him his first wages, in cash. There was a short discussion about where best to find a cheap, secondhand bicycle. The old man drew a rough map and sent him off in the direction of the local council tip, two miles away on top of a ridge. Aspiration counted more than reality, and it had been renamed a Recycling Centre.

The totter presided over her wares seated behind a sliding window set in a snug little container. When business was slack, she pored over an atlas and other books of reference in a doomed attempt to become quiz night queen. When he arrived, he went straight to a pile of bicycles and started to disentangle them. There was a tourer in quite good condition. The frame was adequate and the wheels not buckled although both tyres were flat. The saddle was missing but he found a sprung leather one on another bike, torn and scuffed but serviceable.

He haggled for a while with the totter over at her window. He considered trying to charm her, but saw that it was useless and paid her price.

He wheeled it back to the campsite, as excited by the idea of pedalling about once more as he had been by the arrival of his first child's bike, swathed mysteriously in corrugated paper. He set the tourer upside down outside the office, and borrowed some tools from the old man to remove the wheels and tyres, and repair the inner tubes. It reminded him of his first confident business venture, aged eight, when he and his brother had set up a bicycle repair workshop in an outhouse. They called themselves an unlimited company, because it seemed a shame to be limited in any way. They fixed punctures, painted frames in outrageous colours, and twisted handlebars into impossible angles. Until finally they had to accept that there were no customers for their bizarre customisations.

6.

The pathways to feelgood have been diverted by the centuries of science. The hunter-gatherer could draw energy from bare necessity, from the accomplishment of daily survival. But without the terror and adversity which moulded ancestral minds, the modern pursuit of feelgood is fleeting and frustrated.

Be transport wise, thought the man. Do not fill a fuel tank or pay a fare. The result is too quick, too easy, too unnecessary. Fight instead for every metre of motion, for every crank of the pedals against wind, gradient and fatigue. Reconnect with adversity out in the open and see how good it feels.

That evening, he fried a little bacon to add to his staple rice and vegetable. Cycling around the lanes, with almost no brakes, had rekindled in him his boyhood passion. Exhilaration took hold and never seemed to fade, never even to diminish, dare he think it. Now he could get to places many miles away, and still return home the same day. But not yet. He would have to regain his fitness gradually.

The increase in freedom excited him. He bought bacon as a treat for himself, but he was not the only one to savour its aroma. A forlorn figure appeared at the quarry entrance, holding a front paw off the ground and moving forward with awkward three-legged bounds. At first, in the evening gloom he mistook it for some stray dog, but as it advanced cautiously towards his fire he could see by its head and the length of fur that it was a mink hound.

The first few moments of their meeting established a friendship. The hound's eyes suggested entreaty yet aloofness. His own were amused yet compassionate. He took some bacon from the pan, broke up some bread into a dish, added a little rice and set the food down near the fire. He went over to the spring to collect fresh water in a bowl, which he put down with the food. Then he sat behind the fire, prepared himself a plateful and ate greedily. All the while the hound observed him closely but did not move.

'It may not be much, but it's all I have to offer.'

His tone was gentle and encouraging. Above all confident. It seemed to settle something, for the hound moved forward to the bowls, lapping at the water and catching at mouthfuls of food. He made no attempt to reach out to it. He wondered about the paw. A thorn perhaps, or the vicious bite of a mink. In any case, it was best left for now. When the hound had finished, it collapsed onto its side and lay there, watching him and his movements. How strange, he thought. Dogs and their masters often seemed to look alike. And now this long-legged creature with a shaggy beard and the air of an outsider had found him.

It had been reassured by his voice, so he talked on. He had spoken very little in the last week. He began to rediscover the pleasure of conversation, albeit rather one-sided. He told of his journey there, of his work at the campsite and of his purchase that day. The bicycle stood propped against the quarry wall, its shiny alloy catching the firelight.

" Of course you may be gone by morning and I wouldn't blame you, yet somehow in that state I doubt it. The kennels are miles off, on the other side of the Moor. I heard them discussing the hunt this morning in the village. I could ring up tomorrow and see if they would come for you. But they don't have time for clever hounds that are a nuisance, and stray from the pack. You might end up shot for your trouble.'

He fell silent. He preferred not to wonder out loud how he would be able to manage with another mouth to feed. He might get scraps from the campsite, and he still had the catapult, which so far he had been reluctant to use. With a little practice, he might kill a few vermin.

He grew tired of thinking about it. He built up the fire and climbed into his cave, falling asleep soon after. When he woke during the night to revive the flames, he found the hound sprawled out as before, but breathing quietly.

In the morning it seemed brighter, sitting up and hungry again, he guessed. He fetched water from the spring, then made a large pan of porridge which he shared, stirring in a little honey. He resolved to spend the day in the quarry, trying out the catapult on a target he rigged up on the opposite rockface. He made an area under the awning comfortable for the hound.

All the while it watched him, and licked steadily at its wounded paw. He resisted the temptation to interfere. Instead, he began to think of a name for it. He would need to call it something, to find a word it responded to. It was so silly, the fuss people made about names. Yet the wrong name could hang from you like a dead weight, and slowly pull you down.

'Argus.' He suddenly came out with it. 'I will call you Argus. Never was there a finer or more faithful hound.'
It brought a response. A hesitant little wag of the tail, the first since its arrival. He was pleased with the name, and repeated it several times during the day, each time making the designation clear. By evening Argus seemed recovered, almost eager.

7.

The next morning, he had work to do at the campsite and food to find for the hound. He explained to the old man after work how it had arrived injured at his fireside.

'That'd be you then, would it, up at the clump?'
He was startled to find himself exposed, and so soon. It showed on his face.

'The sisters were asking me who it was living in there. They have the big house on the other side of the hill, and the land thereabouts belongs to them. I guessed it was you and told them so. Used to be an old tramp made a home in the cave up there, but he died more than forty years back. I did most of my courting in the quarry, when I was a lad. But I haven't been back there for a year or two now.'

'Will the owners want me to leave?'

'They never minded about the tramp, so I guess if you're sensible, they'll leave you to it.' The conversation moved on to

17

Argus. The Hunt had looked for him the day after apparently, but it all sounded rather half-hearted. Lie low for a bit, the old man advised, and nothing would come of it. They rustled up some bones and scraps, and there was the promise of more in a few days.

As he cycled back up the hill, standing on the pedals and using his weight to maintain the momentum, he was aware of a lurking anxiety. The idea that Argus might have left during the morning troubled him. The hound was moving about again, albeit lame still, and he might have thought himself abandoned and moved on elsewhere.

Instinct rose up to counter his doubt. A bond existed between himself and Argus, not a collar and lead but a mutual respect and understanding. Their temperaments and their needs coincided. He did not want a pet, but a companion would be welcome in his rehabilitation. Argus must sense that his freedom was unchallenged and that his hunger would be satisfied. The fire as much as anything should hold him in, its flame his gravity. But despite this reasoning, the man was anxious.

The hound heard the bicycle pushing through the undergrowth, and lept ungainly forward in greeting. He knew immediately of the food in the rucksack, and poked at it with his nose. It was a happy reunion.
'Hold on now, let me get myself organised.'
He set down the remains of a leg of lamb and some other scraps. The hound made short work of them. Feeding such a frame would be quite a task. Later he tried hunting in the wood with the catapult. Argus regarded him curiously as he crept about with attempted stealth, missing several rabbits. Eventually he succeeded in bringing down a grey squirrel, which had thought itself safe enough amongst the branches. It lay on the ground motionless, a large nut still held firmly in its mouth. An obol for the squirrel ferry over the Styx.

Argus nudged at the corpse suspiciously. There had been no chase, no excitement and the sport of it was dubious, the quarry too passive.

18

The man picked it up and skinned it with his bowie-knife. They would be hungry again soon enough. At dusk, when the rabbits emerged nervously to graze in the quarry, he positioned himself in careful ambush. The presence of the hound didn't help, and word seemed to have got around that he had rejoined the selfish fray. He had lost the element of surprise, but nevertheless he was confident they would learn to hunt together.

The following day, when he set off with the bicycle, Argus went with him. He thought about trying to discourage this, yet he preferred the hound to decide for himself. Once out on the tarmac he freewheeled and pedalled his way forward sedately, whilst Argus loped alongside. At first he was surprised by how well it worked, until he remembered that hounds regularly went out to exercise this way.

They headed towards the south side of the hill, down past the Georgian house. No sense in being furtive, now that his presence had been discovered. On a vegetable plot beside the road two elderly women were bent over forks, their faces close to the red earth. He waved cheerily, and they straightened to acknowledge his greeting. They were intrigued, and their benign curiosity was framed by the starched white of their wimples. He grinned at the old man's economy. Sisters indeed, but he guessed they were united more by God than by blood.

He kept on down the hill, resolving to wait for his presence to become unremarkable before he stopped to talk to anyone.

He was concerned for Argus, but the hound limped along well enough. It was clear that being out and about after several days of inactivity suited him. His ears were pricked forwards, his manner alert and eager. They both craved movement and novelty.

Time travels faster on a bicycle. Scientific fact. Time is a function of gravity and speed. No mechanical transport is slower or less gravitational than the bicycle. So time speeds up, and the brain senses a relief from banality. Which feels good.

8.

They went down to the campsite together. It was an unusual sight thereabouts, a shaggy minkhound with lambent eyes cantering alongside an equally shaggy man on a bicycle. They turned heads, which was the opposite of his intention. Although he knew it to be foolish, he was caught up in the pleasure of his new friendship and to hell with the consequences. Joy had been hard to come by of late, so he decided to relax his discipline and try a little self-indulgence.

Argus was a success with the campers. The old man admired the hound and welcomed his presence. During the cleaning and tidying chores, Argus sniffed and wagged his way about, fed and fussed over. When the old mower spluttered into life, he barked and chased it up and down the stripes.

They visited the Recycling Centre to find a rack to fix over the rear wheel of the bicycle. That way the man could relieve his back of the weight of the rucksack. There was no question of trying to charm the totter. Argus did so effortlessly, and they came away only a pound the poorer. In return he had a rear rack and an ancient pair of canvas panniers. They were ripped in places, and the buckles missing, but with the help of a strong plastic bag inside each one and some string as fastener, he was equipped to travel with confidence. And how he felt on a bicycle made all the difference to how willingly his legs cranked the pedals. The secret was to blank off from the brain the whole of the upper body, letting hands and arms relax, and to visualise only from the hips down. This concentrated all the energy where it was most needed. Another trick he had was to think of something rather wonderful when he saw a hill up ahead, and to distract himself with the wonder of it until he reached the top. By that time the pain and the effort were past and somehow unrecorded.

It was a vision to gladden the heart of any passer-by and pull a smile across a face. Argus moved in his recovery from limp to lope to canter and finally to bound. He relished the speed of their travel, especially on the flat or downhill. His head was held high, almost level with the handlebars, his ears thrown back, his muzzle a grin and the rest of his body sprung with movement.

Alongside, the man sat upright in the saddle, the better to look about and see over the hedges. He gazed at fields of emerging corn, at herds of cattle released from their winter sheds, at farmsteads burrowed into folds of land. The whip of the spring air brought tears to his eyes and a drip to his nose. Never had he known such a feeling of present purpose. Whereas in truth they moved quite aimlessly along the lanes, for the pleasure of discovery and displacement.

9.

Two walkers whose paths cross have ample time to assess one another, perchance to meet and share a greeting or a flash of camaraderie.

By contrast two cyclists travelling the same road from opposite directions have but a fraction of time to exchange impressions. Unsatisfactory, in the way that only the impression lingers, whilst the detail fizzes at the edge of memory and is gone. Yet delicious in the intensity and drama of the snapshot.

When the man slowed one day to approach a bend, and called Argus closer to his wheels, he had only the briefest of moments to notice the girl cycling towards him. He saw her brake and then wobble, distracted from her line by Argus' movements. And then she recovered her balance and looked up. For an instant, their eyes locked and their lives aligned, before momentum carried them helplessly on and away.

She wondered who would have the honesty and the daring to disturb the universe at such a point. To brake to a sudden halt and shout 'Stop!' over the shoulder. Stop. I haven't seen enough, and if I don't detonate this moment's charge, I may never see enough. I may live forever with the flash of a sepia face and a sense of unfulfilled excitement.

She thought how often she had passed an interesting turning, one which revealed a beautiful vista or which spoke of an intriguing diversion. More often than not she would stop, retrace her steps and pursue the distraction, however purposeful her original course. Yet whenever such encounters involved another person, she found herself paralysed by the crush of consequence. It was easy enough to interact with the natural world, to flirt casually with its beauty and then turn away. Shut a door, draw a curtain, even forget, without fear of reprisal. Not so easy with people, when the smack of a kiss could set off a smothering avalanche of emotional endeavour.

The natural world certainly inspired her with love, a love which was free of complication and commitment. But she was aware of a snag, one which she remembered from reading Turgenev. Nature inspired love, but couldn't satisfy it. And there was no doubting that the brain demanded love, demanded to love and be loved. With a flow of love and information, the brain would cease its bellowing, and ruminate in contentment.

10.

She freewheeled down the hill towards the bridge. She liked to pause there, and still astride her bicycle she would lean against the stone parapet and look over at the river. Beside it ran the railway, accompanying the swirling waters for nearly 50 miles on their journey to the sea. It was a single track branch line, entwining itself about the river and the road again and again, with tunnels and endless bridges of stone and steel, until finally they both disgorged together at the ancient seaport. The railway was a lucky survivor of the cuts, but regularly someone brandished a sword and threatened to slice off the serpent's head.

She liked to watch for the compact little two-carriage trains which beat their way up and down. They travelled so slowly you could glimpse the passengers inside, seated at tables or reclining back. She imagined their lives, and their stories, just as she did lying in bed when the North wind brought the iron horse beat to her cottage windows.

Whilst crossing over the river, there was a remarkable geological transition. On one side, she admired the open sweep of the fertile red land. Big country, with its expanse of arable fields and its vast skies. It contained the spewings of an ancient volcano, which had attracted men and their industrious ploughs ever since.

Yet she preferred the other side, a land of heavy clay, steeply wooded coombs and clinging pasture. A land alien to the plough and mechanical invention. A land of privacy and secrets and mystery. Here in this coy world she had made herself a home.

For two miles she cycled along a tributary of the river, working her way gently uphill until the curtain of trees and terrain closed behind her. West of the lane was an ancient farmstead, which a prosperous yeoman had gentrified. A substantial house was set on a hill above the farm buildings. Four cottages had once been spread apart over the land to house labourers and their families. They had been scooped into sheltered spots, built of subsoil from the site to make cob walls and wheat straw from the fields to make thatch.

During the agricultural depression the farm had been split up and the cottages abandoned. The others had long since dissolved, but hers she had made to live again. It was set east of the lane in a little wooded coomb, watered by its own stream and defended all about by forty acres of its own land.

A stone track led up through woods for a ¼ mile, emerging suddenly into a bright clearing. Here above the stream on a south-facing bank was a small terraced area, large enough to accommodate a stone and cob cottage, a barn, a garden and a gravelled turning area. It was a compact set-up, ideally designed for the refugee, the outsider. She could spend days on end there and not see another person.

She made her way up the track, pushing the bicycle over the uneven surface of stones. She had learnt from experience that the spokes of her wheels tended to break if she rode over the rough ground, especially when laden with shopping. She had quick-fitting panniers made of strong black nylon, into which were piled all her groceries and shopping when she visited the town. The bicycle was her only means of transport, and it took her as far as the railway station when she ventured further than legs could take her.

The land supplied many of her needs. Timber for building and fencing. Plentiful firewood for heating and cooking. Vegetables and fruit from the garden. Water from the stream and from a spring which rose out of the bank behind the barn. There was no electricity from the mains grid. The cottage had never been connected, but she used solar panels to recharge batteries instead. Her annual expenses were negligible. A few thousand pounds for the food she couldn't grow, her clothes, the telephone connection and other luxuries. And the land even supplied those, albeit indirectly, from the money she received selling the annual grazing rights to her fields.

It was not so much an ecological conviction which led her to live this way, although she didn't trouble to correct anyone who suggested such a motive. Rather it was her resolve to live independently of others, and not be subject to their whims, inefficiencies and unreliability. She believed in the idea of responsibility, and the more she found those around her happy to deny theirs, the more she acknowledged her own.

Neither was it conviction which made her diet vegetarian, but rather down to earth practicality. She didn't have enough power to run a fridge, and without one keeping meat was troublesome. There were those who assumed conviction in both cases. Being unashamed to be identified in that way she never bothered to contradict their assumptions. In truth she was suspicious of most forms of evangelism. She found its effects tiresome and restrictive, and resolved to keep her own counsel.

11.

Some said she had the ideal place to develop a smallholding, but she knew her heart wasn't in it. In the same way that she sought independence for herself, so she avoided dependence in others. She loved to see her fields full of well-fed sheep or cattle. There was nothing more picturesque than sheep standing stock still and apart in the teeming rain, or lain down together beneath the canopy of a great oak. Nothing more reassuring than the soft, languid movements of the cows, with their gentle, inquisitive eyes. She delighted in their presence, but was pleased that someone else took care of their needs.

If she kept hens, she would have fresh eggs. She would also have the headache of their wilful gardening, and the heartache of the fox's vendetta. She preferred to encourage the pheasants, which roosted wild in the trees and foraged for themselves in the woods.

She could have had geese to guard her home and decorate her pond, but their incessant chatter and a gander's aggression would soon depress her spirits, and she chose rather to enjoy the distant honking of the wild geese when they flew overhead. Sometimes they honoured her with a visit to the pond, and she was spellbound to see them stacked up on their landing flightpath like passenger jets.

She might have had a dog for company and protection, but she abhorred the fawning dependence of so many pets. She preferred to make the wildlife surrounding her cottage confident enough to wander at will. The roe deer grew to accept her scent, and would graze furtively on the lawn at dusk, whilst she watched from an open window. The hares set her giggling with their ridiculous comings and goings, and the badgers dramatised the night with their disputes.

Her greatest pleasure was to be woken from her sleep by the hoot or the screech of an owl perched in the tree above her skylight. Or to turn over and find the room flooded with moonlight. At times, she wondered whether others would admire the simplicity of her life, or pity its sterility.

She ought to have had a cat, to catch the cohorts of mice which favoured the cottage with their endless scuttlings, scratchings and gnawings. But then how would she bear it when the cat hunted the songbirds, the most delicate and enchanting of her wild companions? She put out copious quantities of peanuts, seeds and other food for them throughout the winter, and was rewarded at dawn and at dusk with a music whose equal she never found on a recording or a radio concert.

She dawdled in bed the morning after her cycling encounter with the man and his dog. The spring months were the finest by far for birdsong, when the maelstrom of courtship and territorial defence blended into a sublime whirlpool of song. She thought that now hope and nascent energy were so strong in the natural world, it almost compensated for the unrequited love which it inspired. Almost. For the vision of man and dog wouldn't leave her. It kept reminding her of something which was missing.

She had never seen them before, and she travelled on most of the local lanes for the sake of variety. They had to be new to the area, or just passing through, but they didn't have the manner or the look of itinerants. The man had the proprietorial air of a local, and as for the dog, she couldn't remember ever having seen such a one before. It looked like some sort of hunting dog, and as she pictured it she smiled at the memory of its tousy good nature. It was remarkable enough to meet another cyclist, outside the summer holidays. Especially one who cycled for transport as opposed to those who did so for fun, usually on a Sunday. Even more remarkable for it to be a strange looking man, accompanied by such a dog.

She began to understand why their image stayed with her, and why it seemed to excite her. She might spend the rest of her life bicycling her solitary way about and never in all those years would she be likely to have an experience even vaguely similar to that of yesterday.

She sat up suddenly in bed. What tricks the mind played. You could go about your daily business, and when something extraordinary happened, your brain would pass it off as just another piece of information, processed and filed accordingly. It was only when you demanded to see the file again, that you realised the true nature of the event.

She dressed and set about her morning ritual. Spring's optimism suffused her body, and dimly she was aware of a link between her seasonal excitement and yesterday's encounter. She diverted her energy into the garden, preparing the ground for vegetables and the greenhouse for early planting. She cut the lawn. There was no pleasure for her in the act of mowing, but she enjoyed the way the grass responded. Never did it allow you to get the better of it, never would it give up, not even after frost.

She walked to the top of the hill behind the cottage and looked out northwards. She could see in the distance the beginning of the plough land, its redness the blood of industry.

12.

It was the time of year for selling the annual grazing rights to her land. For the last few years a neighbouring farmer had been pleased to buy them. He didn't have enough land of his own to feed a large flock of Suffolk sheep and a motley herd of beef cattle. It suited him to have his animals close by, and although better grassland could be had further off, convenience outweighed quality.

Trust counted too. Amongst the many business disciplines, farming was the one to make long term thought instinctive. Farmers stayed put, working the same land from one generation to another, so that their investment might be everlasting. The same applied to maintaining good relations with suppliers and customers. The short-term dogma of the modern market was alien to them.

She knew that the farmer trusted her. She always kept an eye on the animals on her land, and told him promptly of any problems. Nevertheless, she remained apprehensive. Selling the grazing was her one significant source of income. And she preferred to deal with someone she knew, someone whose visits to check on the stock throughout the summer would not be intrusive.

She telephoned and he came over to walk the land and discuss terms. He had the large round face of an owl, and the same shrewd, slightly startled look. They examined the state of the fencing along her boundaries. It was always a case of patch and mend, for she never had the means to make a proper job of it.

They agreed a price, conditional on her repairing several stretches which were weak enough to invite escape. They shook hands on the deal, and she felt with pleasure the callused glove of hard labour, and the gentle power lurking beneath.

She took on the outside work herself, not to prove to others or even to herself her capability, but rather to be free of the nightmare of dependence. Better by far to take several hours or even several days longer than a professional to get the job done, when the alternative might involve waiting hours or days for someone to turn up. When they did arrive, she couldn't trust that the work would be properly done. Then she still had to go out to work to earn the money to pay their bill. Better to sweep aside the whole tottering pyramid of dependence. Simply do it yourself.

She had pulled a wheelbarrow for miles during the cottage renovations, seeking building stone from the fields and the stream in order to repair the crumbling walls. She had mixed tons of lime mortar by hand with a shovel, and plastered much of it over the cob and stone inside to make a practical finish. She had become adept at sawing, drilling, screwing and nailing timber of all kinds, and all sizes. In this way she had woven herself into the fabric of the cottage, and it had secreted its dust deep in her lungs. The bond between them was as strong as any she knew, and it constituted the greater part of her sense of belonging, her sense of rightfulness and well-being.

She knew and accepted her physical limitations. Previous efforts had taught her that some of the tasks of fencing were beyond her. Wielding an iron bar to make holes in the ground, heaving a sledgehammer high above the head to knock stakes deep into the earth, lifting the great rolls of wire netting, these things she counted as beyond her strength.

There was a man in the village who made a part time living from such work. She had called for his help before on a few occasions. She resolved to cycle that way at lunchtime, and knock at his bungalow to ask for a day's fencing from him.

She might have telephoned, but she preferred the excuse it gave to go out on the bicycle, a destination in mind. The time was ideal for cycling, the air warm enough by midday but never stifling, never without the tinge of freshness which sparkled in the countryside all about.

She called in at the Post Office on her way, to buy milk and bread. It was there that her second encounter with the man and his dog took place. As she opened the door to leave, he was about to come in. Each blocked the way forward of the other. Instead of the customary apologies and side steps, there was silence and no attempt to make room. They simply stood and stared, not from conscious decision, but because for the three or four seconds of their meeting, their brains crashed through the floor of the everyday into a cellar of furtive imaginings.

Argus came to the rescue. His attempt to push past into the shop forced the man to react, grabbing the hound and moving sideways towards the phonebox. She went over to her bicycle and set off for home, completely forgetting the errand which had brought her there. She knew instinctively that the man's eyes were locked onto her movements. Her scalp tingled, and she felt the purest, most intense release of joy.

13.

The girl was so troubled by the encounter, she travelled more than a mile before coming to her senses. She was aware that something was making a regular metallic knock, and then she wondered if this was related to the discomfort in her saddle. Eventually she came to a stop and noticed, without the usual dark mutterings, that her bike had a flat tyre.

She was surprised at how easy it was to dismount and continue at a walk, without it affecting her high spirits. She was surprised at how inevitable it seemed when Argus appeared from nowhere, and thrust his muzzle between her legs by way of greeting and friendship.

The man arrived soon afterwards. He had spent five minutes seated on a bench by the phonebox, debating violently with himself what to do. Rational good sense told him to keep away, to continue to spend his time quiet and alone. At the same time, a sap rose in him as it rose in the natural world all about him, after the dark, bleak incarceration of winter. The life force would not be held back. It pushed weeds up through thick concrete and it propelled him towards the girl in a priapic trance of hope.

He leant his bicycle against a gate and took hers from her, gently but without question. He upended it at the side of the lane, released the wheel from the frame and began to inspect the tyre. Then he produced levers from inside his panniers, and removed the tyre and its tube from the wheel.

His movements were so clean, confident and precise. She sat on the opposite bank and watched. She was fascinated by an operation which would normally bore her to distraction.

He pumped up the inner and held it to his ear, listening for the tell-tale hiss of escape. He covered an area with glue from a small tube, and holding it out to dry he looked up and across at her. Still neither of them spoke, but his face betrayed his amusement. His eyes were creased and narrowed in laughter, his mouth open and his lips pulled back.

Her own smile in reply was timid and restrained, almost sly. She began to relax and enjoy this mime of courtship, this wordless dance. She fell in with his unspoken request not to break the spell with words, heavy, clumsy, worn-out words. Their communication was the electric charge in the air between them. Enjoy it whilst it lasts, he seemed to suggest, enjoy it whilst the electrons of nowness and newness discharge themselves. Later we can fall back on the humdrum loom of language.

He handed back her bicycle, the puncture now repaired. She set off again, and he cycled alongside, uninvited and not unwelcome. Argus seemed delighted to have two machines to frustrate, as he crossed and recrossed in front of them on his erratic scentings. They glided down the lane alongside a river, beneath a closing canopy of oak, ash and beech . They were both sensible of the pleasure of togetherness, and the relief of companionship. The effort compared to solo cycling was reduced because the brain was occupied elsewhere.

After a few miles, she turned off up a farm track and dismounted. He followed suit. They wheeled their bicycles along the bottom of a steep-sided, wooded coomb. A stream cut a rapid channel towards them, and a long thin pond had been dug beside it. Argus bounded in without hesitation, and then began to hunt his way up the bed of the stream.

They emerged into a clearing and he had a first sight of the buildings. There was a very patched and repaired cottage, looking south across a private little valley. The roof had been renewed. It held two skylights and was covered in cedar shingles which had begun to turn a silvery grey. The front door and some of the windows were made of ancient weatherbeaten oak. A barn was set at a rightangle to the west of the cottage, forming a little courtyard and turning its back on the stormy southwesterlys. The large barn doors stood open to the east, showing an ancient lorry, stacks of firewood, piles of timber and other building materials. There was a workshop bench placed beneath a large unglazed opening.

The effect of the whole was reassuring and protective. First the valley held them in, and blocked out the prying world beyond. The trees were magnificent, thriving on the heavy soil and the mild, sheltered micro climate. Some of the more ancient oaks stood alone as mutely stationed sentinels. Then the little courtyard of buildings embraced them warmly, shutting out the wind and rain but taking the full heat of the sun. Some visionary had planted a Scots Pine in the bank behind the cottage. It held itself to attention with an evergreen umbrella unfurled against attack from the air.

They propped their cycles inside the barn. He stood back and gazed at it all, whilst she sat on a wooden bench beside the cottage door, and watched him gaze.

She went inside to heat some water to make tea. When she came out, he was still standing in the same spot, turning slowly to record in detail his surroundings. The lay energy travelled up through his body from the earth, and shone in his face.

She brought out a tray of tea, with slices of fresh bread and her homemade jam. He joined her on the bench, and sipped tea between mouthfuls. It felt as if the sun was setting on their meeting. Its heat and concentration left them drained and lightheaded. She spoke first, to break a silence which had lasted from the beginning.

'I envy you. I shall never see it again for the first time. Never with fresh eyes, from afar, like you. I shall always be too close.'

'May I come here again? I was thinking second time the effect might be as strong. Undiminished.'

'There's some fencing I have to do this week. Please come again. Tomorrow if you like. You can help me with it.'

He nodded his agreement, thanked her for the tea, and set off down the track, nursing his battered bicycle over the bumpy surface, whilst Argus raced ahead.

14.

'When the Normans came here, they called the place Charrafin. Not for what it is, but for what it isn't. When they found the fertile redlands there to the north, they colonised them and set their greedy ploughs to work. Here you can still sense their disappointment, as they fell off the redland into clay, and clung miserably to the sharp valleys. It was too steep even for a hunting forest. For them, it was simply "the end of the ploughland".'

They were working in the top field, setting out stakes where they were needed, and rolling out the wire netting. He made holes for the rough oak timbers, hewn from her own woodland, and knocked them into the earth until they were firm. She came behind, and fixed the wire to them with staples. From the field, they could see north as far as the neat rectangular patchwork and treeless sweep of the ploughland, as well as south to the monstrous humpback silhouette of the Moor.

'I first came here by accident really, heading elsewhere. I saw the auctioneer's 'For Sale' board, and carried on past on my way to visit a friend. But the image of that board, nailed to a beech tree at the end of the lane, wouldn't leave me. I cannot account for the force that brought me back the next day. Partly curiosity of course, but also an unseen hand, tugging at my sleeve.'

'Did you know the name by then?'

'No, I still had no idea what was for sale. I had to fight my way up the track, it was so overgrown. I remember feeling confident, and not at all discouraged. Euphoric. I knew before I even reached the ruins that something really good was about to be revealed. It's one of the few times I've ever had that excited feeling of certainty.'

They were sitting on the grass now to rest, looking down a steep wooded incline to the back of the cottage. Because it was burrowed into the bank, only the upper storey was visible, camouflaged by its roof of shingles. Woodsmoke gathered in idle puffs around the chimney on a still, serene day.

'It was about this time of year. I remember there was no clearing then. The ash trees had seeded themselves all over, and grown up around the buildings to shade them from the world. There were no doors, the place had just been abandoned to the elements and the creatures of the wood. I frightened some roe deer. I remember how they barked, they were so cross at being disturbed. Yet I didn't feel myself to be an intruder. I was so sure, even then, that this would be my home.'

He lay back on the grass and rested his head lightly on the sprawled, sleeping body of Argus. He had no home, but it didn't seem to trouble him. For the time being, he would remain a rootless vagabond, ready to move at a moment's notice. The romance of it appealed to him. He pictured the end of 'The Searchers'. He wondered when he too would crave a rocking chair on a veranda.

'I went into the auctioneer's office in town to get some information about the place. They were more used to dealing with locals. I could see the agent thinking what's this doe-eyed dreamer doing wasting my time. I persevered. Eventually they gave me a page of typed details with no photograph. It was then that I noticed the name. I knew what it meant. I sat down there in the office, and burst into tears. To everyone's confusion and discomfort. Then I pulled myself back together, stood up and said "I'll buy it". There must have been something in the way I said it, because straightaway the auctioneer took me seriously. He told me later it was one of the strangest sales he's ever made. Still now when I see him in town, he grins sheepishly and gives me a wide berth.'

He laughed. It was the first time she had seen him relax his guard so far. They went down to the barn and walked back up with the last of the stakes and some netting. They were happy in their work, well satisfied with the progress they had made. The day was blissful. They were easy in each other's company. There was such a shared understanding between them, they felt as if they had been friends for a long time.

He thought about her story of how she came to be here. There seemed to be a piece missing.

'What was it about the name Charrafin that made you cry?'

She was bending over a stake, trying to hammer the staples into the iron heartwood without bending them. The only way was to find a fault or a split in the wood, and hammer home into the weakness.

She looked up, first at him, then beyond him towards her past. For a while, she didn't reply and he began to feel he had delved too far.

'After the scene with the auctioneer, I went straight back to London. At that time, I owned a little terraced house, on a large estate. They mostly belonged to one of the big London housing charities, but they were being sold off when the tenants died. I remember camping out overnight on the pavement in front of the estate office to be sure of getting one. It took me ages to renovate the inside, it was in such a state of disrepair. Anyway, I went back and I sold it. There was no delay. Those houses were so much in demand, people fought over them. I handed in my notice at work. I bought the old lorry, the one in the barn, at a council auction. It had been fitted out as a mobile library, with beautifully made wooden shelving for the books, and skylights that opened. I piled in all my things, and I drove down here. I parked the lorry in the yard, and I lived in it quite happily that summer whilst I got on with renovating the cottage.'

She had followed her own thread into a maze of memory, and for the moment it seemed as if she had lost sight of the starting point. He asked no more and began to prepare holes for the last of the stakes. He was surprised when suddenly she began again.

'In my job, I went where I was directed, and I did as I was instructed. I worked in order to live in London, and to pay the bills. It was a good enough way to be, privileged even. But the greater part of that life was not really my own. I was just so much ploughland, to be passively cultivated and sown to the advantage of others, at their bidding. I was desperate to break free, to live and decide for myself. I cried because it was too wonderful. I had been given the chance I sought, led to it even. It put me where I wanted to be, beyond the plough.'

15.

When the work was finished, she brought up the subject of wages. How much an hour should she pay him? He didn't want to accept any money. It might disrupt the nature of their new friendship. He suggested that an invitation to supper would balance the debt. She agreed, and set about cooking something from the limited ingredients she had to hand.

The truth was, he needed to gain himself more time. So far, she had asked no questions of his life. She had every reason to be confident and at ease in his company, or so she made clear. His weaker nature devoured such a presumption. He found himself forever putting off the moment when he must reveal his recent past and risk losing her good opinion, perhaps even her friendship.

He left it until after supper, until he was cornered. No more time. He swallowed, and threw himself into it.

'Do you know the clump? The old quarry in the woodland behind the Sisters' house?'

'I have heard of it, but I've never seen in there. It always looks so overgrown and impenetrable.'

'That's where we're living, Argus and me.'

He looked down at the hound, quite at home lying beside the hearth. He was awake and watchful, alerted either by mention of his name, or by the strained nature of the man's voice.

'We're both fugitives, you see. Outsiders. Deserted in his case, he decided to leave the pack. I was excluded. For seven years. In prison.'

'So you're on parole?'

The question surprised him. It was not what he expected, and it was fired back at him with little reaction or hesitation on her part.

'No. I served my full sentence.'

'Then you have paid your debt, haven't you.'

It occurred to him that she must somehow have known, or guessed, the truth. She betrayed no surprise. He plunged on, while he still dared.

'My conviction was for manslaughter. For some people, justice demands a life for a life.'

Still no change in her demeanour.

'I was careful when I came to the quarry to leave no trace. They won't have found me yet, but I feel sure they're looking. The word will be out, and they can afford to pay a generous bounty.'

This time, he got a reaction. She turned away towards the sink, to hide her face, and became busy there. He thought he should leave. He had said enough. But he must spell it out, for his own peace of mind.

'I shouldn't have allowed myself to follow you, yesterday. I'm sorry. In the future, every time you are seen with me, you are potentially in danger. Potentially a target. They might use anything to get at me.'

Leave now. He stood up. Argus had been watching them, and he too scrabbled up. She was still standing at the sink, looking out of the window past its eroded oak mullions into the fading light of dusk. He opened the front door, and reached over to touch her hand gently.

'Thank you for supper. It's been the best day for me in more than seven years. Goodbye.'

Then they were gone. He hurtled down the track, careless of his own safety, or the bicycle's. Speed and movement, to clear the head and rinse through the emotions. The twilight was his excuse to cycle flat out along the lanes, and to stand up on the pedals to attack the hills. It was exhilarating. Argus caught his mood and responded with his own distracted sprint. His limp was gone, and the lithesome grace of his gallop highlighted the comic curl of his whiskers and the kink of his ear lugs.

16.

The funk he felt in the following days threatened to overwhelm him. The remedy was obvious. It was time to set about his preparations. When he wasn't working down at the campsite, he began to dig a pit. From many idle moments spent looking at the quarry, he reasoned that there was only one practical way in. The one in that he used himself. The only other way would be to tie a rope to a tree up on the rim and abseil down. It was too steep and difficult to find a path down, too far to jump. The likelihood of an attacker being sufficiently skilled and equipped to abseil seemed negligible, and in any case since he couldn't defend against it, there was little point in worrying about it.

He concentrated his energies where it made most sense. He would dig a trap where the path narrowed. A hephalump trap. A covering of rotten branches could support the camouflage of leaves and turf and ferns, but give way beneath the weight of an intruder.

He borrowed a pick and a shovel from the campsite. He used his bivi-bag as a wheelbarrow, piling the earth on top of it, then sliding it downhill through the wood to dispose of the soil out of sight.

The work was hard, but therapeutic. For as long as he worked, he didn't think of the girl. In the evenings, he was tired, after preparing a meal for himself. It prevented his mind obsessing in the grinding, gormless way it favoured on such occasions.

He slept lightly, as he had taught himself to do. He woke at regular intervals, to feed the fire and listen.

He cycled into town one day. It was dangerous, but necessary. He couldn't take Argus, that would attract far too much attention, so he shut him in the mower shed, and cycled off to howls of indignity. It was the first time he had treated the hound that way, and he hated doing so.

It didn't take long to buy nylon rope, jumbo-sized cable ties, a disposable flash camera and strong black adhesive tape. And some tins of dog food. He didn't like to visit the gossipy butcher's shop for bones and scraps.

On his return, he was greeted by a mink hound sulk, which lasted all of thirty seconds. Coincidentally thirty seconds was how long it took to find a tin opener and empty out the contents on the ground.

His pit had to be at least two metres deep. Anyone who fell in might survive the fall uninjured, but they would lose the initiative. Timing would be essential. The pit would give him, if it worked according to its design, a few seconds to seize the initiative for himself and overpower any assailant. He was unarmed, whereas his opponent would certainly use a firearm. The pit was conceived to momentarily disarm.

Of course, if he was prepared to do harm in the interests of self-defense, his planning would be more straightforward. He might drive stakes into the floor of the trap, for instance, and then sharpen the ends into lethal points. Anyone who fell in would be skewered.

This was not an option. He must overpower and temporarily disable his attacker, without doing him serious bodily harm. It would complicate matters if the police had reason to pursue him. He had no desire to spend any more of his life inside. The law allowed him to use reasonable force to defend himself, but even if his assailant clearly intended to kill him, he was not entitled to kill in self-defense.

It was also not an option because he had no desire to do harm. He was stirred by no feeling of hatred, or revenge. Whoever came for him would most likely be a complete stranger, doing a job in exchange for financial reward. It was not his place to harm or punish such a person. Rather he must use his brain to outwit the opponent and put himself beyond reach.

As well as two metres deep, the pit needed to be more than a stride across, in order to be sure of catching a footfall. Also it had to cut sufficiently across the track that no-one could walk around it. This design meant moving a large amount of earth and stone, much of which was compacted by centuries of quarry traffic. Finally, the walls must be vertical, or even slightly undercut. Not sloping. It was essential that once in, it was a hard struggle to get out.

He relished his task, and the fitness it encouraged in him. Before his digging sessions, he wound the black tape around his fingers to prevent blisters. He set himself targets, and isolated his mind from distraction until they were achieved. He knew it might prove worthless. A drive-by shooting on a lonely stretch of road was just as likely, or a sniper's bullet fired by an unseen hand. But the value of the pit was just as much in what it did for him now, as in what it might do to save him later. First he had decided to stand his ground here, and if he survived he would buy himself time to move discreetly to another position. Whilst he waited at least he had something to do.

17.

The longer days and warmer weather brought an increase in traffic at the campsite. The old man emerged from his office den to welcome his regulars or to quiz newcomers with artful subtlety. His door was left open during the day. From an ancient half-round office chair, covered in leather as tan and parched as his skin, he surveyed the comings and goings of his fiefdom with indulgent curiosity.

He kept a careful record every year of arrivals and departures, noting them down in black-bound A4 diaries. They stood in chronological piles on the floor, on top of which he laid an old pine door for a desk. He consulted the previous year's notes whenever there was a new arrival, so that he always knew the names of parents, children and dogs. He knew what work people did, where they lived and when they drove a new car.

He sauntered, never intrusively, and with a casual remark or a gift of local produce he made his visitors feel special. Many returned year after year in search of these moments. It was so trivial, and yet whenever they spoke of their camping holiday, in retrospect or in anticipation, they spoke of the old man's rustic charm and kindliness.

Their worlds of work and family, town and city, were hectic and in search of reprieve. They found it for a few days each year, camped on a clean, bright lawn beside a meandering sandy river. A village and shop to hand, miles of field, wood and lane all around. A trip in the car if it rained. However they spent their time, the old man's lurking presence was catalytic in their joy. He had always been there, he would always be there, as monumental as the ancient oak tree which dominated the site and drew them in beneath its protective branches.

More visitors meant more cleaning, and more warmth, more grass. The man cycled down from the quarry to begin his chores at the point when most people had completed their breakfast rituals and were off for a morning's entertainment. He was hard pressed to complete the work within the allotted few hours. The old man noted any overtime and paid him accordingly. With this income, and so few expenses, he had begun to put a little money aside for the emergency. He thought with the definite article, because he knew the ordeal was ahead. He had made his plan to stand and fight, and fear alone would not induce him to change it.

He was friendly with the campers, yet he remained a forbidding figure with his long hair and unkempt beard. They found him unapproachable, quite unlike his employer. Meanwhile Argus was aloof with all the other dogs, but he soon found that a little canine charm worked wonders with their masters. This further enraged the dogs, who protested loudly at the success of their rival's wiles.

When the man watched the young children play excitedly on their bicycles, thirty years of his life came away like an itchy, crusty scab to expose the fresh pink of his own youth. The vanity of his efforts since then was revealed to him. The fall of adulthood was not so much a loss of moral innocence, for in many ways he retained that quality, and always would. It was rather the loss of philosophical innocence which he bemoaned. When he had played on his bicycle as the children did still, he could never have suspected that his life would be haunted by the vanity and futility of things. But that spectre of emptiness did not overwhelm him. He recognised the fun and pleasures to be had. Still now, when he gave himself over to the motion and rigour of the bicycle he was transported back to a time and a place akin to his childhood campsite, and to a mood of suspended diminution.

One day in the office, the old man showed him a diary of thirty years back. In it was marked the arrival of his family at the site, alongside his name and that of his brother. There was a note a few days later recording their disappearance. The old man was smiling.

'I remember you said at the start that you'd stayed here as a lad. Then when I heard you were living up at the quarry, I kept thinking there was a memory just out of my reach. Of course, when I saw the entry, it all came back to me. Your parents were so full of guilt and worry at losing you. Everybody was out looking round the village, shouting and calling your names. We thought you might be hiding, just to make a game of it. Then all of a sudden, you both appear down the hill on your bikes, big grins on your faces. So pleased you were with your taste of freedom.'

The old man's eyes glistened. Not at him, but out towards the entrance gate, where they could see again two small figures on their bikes returning in triumph.

'How your parents laid into you, they'd been so worried. Myself, I felt it was a shame you had to be punished. You two were always so easy, so natural in your mischief.'
For a while, they were both lost in separate worlds.

The old man looked back. He thought how if you stayed put long enough, and embraced things, somehow you became a hub around which life revolved. A boy arrived, trouble in tow, and then he came again thirty years later and you couldn't help feeling trouble wasn't far behind.

The man looked back. It was strange that he had no memory of punishment. Only the glow of daring adventure remained. And the wonder of togetherness. He and his brother had been a team, a company, a force to take on the world, confident, undaunted. Never would one betray the other, or let the other down.

And the man looked forward. Now so many years later he was on his own. Round two in the quarry, he would face the unknown alone. Except that a quiet voice in his head said otherwise, said that they were still a team, still a force to be reckoned with. Together.

18.

For as long as he moved on his feet, he was in direct contact with the weight of the world. The earth pinned him down jealously, and each footfall was a jarred reminder of its dominion.

When he moved astride his bicycle, this gravity and depression fell away, releasing him into an exhilarated world of boyhood adventure. If he set out on foot without directions or destination, he was lost and tired and burdened with the absence of his necessity. If he set out cycling, there might be no fixed co-ordinates. He did not reason the need, the suspension of diminution was need enough. For as long as he glided and pedalled and forced a path through the wind, the rushing of the air filled his ears and made him deaf to the grumblings of his own vanity.

Once more he found himself cycling alongside the girl, Argus a tantivy between then. She had left him a note at the campsite office, suggesting they meet at the granite cross beneath the mangled oak tree. Let's cycle from there to the Moor for a picnic, she wrote.

A bicycle, a picnic, a bright June day deep in countryside, Argus and the girl to share with – he smiled to think that all his appetites were united and satisfied, concentrated into one beam of joy. He was aware how much this day would sustain him in the future, but to his credit he didn't only squirrel away its memory. He was so relaxed, he stumbled into the present as well and breathed there quietly for a while.

They travelled at first through a familiar landscape. South through deep and secret valleys of woodland and water, here and there an isolated cottage beside the lane, or the beginning of a farm track. Each entranceway called the curious with its promise of history and beauty and lifelong endeavour. Each turning was an agony of choice, for every way spoke of new adventure. The crossways were haunted by the traffic of centuries and the passion of itinerant preachers. The rivers flowed over the roads on ancient cobbled fords. No haughty bridges to keep the feet dry and set man above nature. There was no sweep to the view, no way to see the elevation of that country, or how it sat in its surroundings. The natural world was there under your nose, in your face and all around you. Either live and breathe it, or be afraid and oppressed.

After an hour's cycling, the succession of valleys gave way to one long ascent up onto the plateau of the Moor. They ground down into their lowest gears, and the rapid pumping of their knees made the slowness of their progress seem ridiculous. The effort might have outweighed the reward, had they not been able to see, for the first time, the nature of the ravined, ploughless forest from which they h₵ emerged.

There be dragons.

Ancient civilisations had fled this way, up onto the Moor, onto its sculpted granite back where they made their camps and compounds. They could see all around to defend themselves, until the fog breathed their animation to a standstill. They celebrated in places where the energy of life rose from the earth like steam and boiled away their fear.

The cycle party fought its way up to the high ground. Perspiration ran from their foreheads and stung their eyes. Their backs were damp with it, yet it was pleasure not pain which registered on their faces as they encouraged each other along. The pleasure of a good sweat, the delight of warm muscles working hard and sound lungs filling again and again with the mossy air.

Once on top, they paused for a while at a viewpoint and drank deeply from their water bottles. Ahead was the rolling open expanse of moorland. Here and there were great dimples in the rock, where water and mud gathered to form fathomless bogs. Elsewhere in shallow coombs, trees grew bent and stooped as old men, blasted and withered by weather and time. Plantations showed up awkwardly alongside, where man insisted on his harvest. Straight rows of conifers crowded upwards, forming sanctuaries of lifeless brown, free from sound and light.

Argus was suddenly a dreamer. His nose pulled in the wind, and what he found captured there made him gaze mysteriously towards the centre.

They followed narrow lanes bordered by endless streams. The roads were open onto moorland either side, with no hedge or bank to break the view. It was so unlike the country they had just crossed. Here there were vistas in all directions. They turned to absorb each new impression.

They grew hungry, and stopped on flat, spongy turf beside a broad stream. The grass had been cropped clean by the sheep and dried out by the sun. They sat on the bank, their feet soothed in cool water. They ate bread and bananas and jam. Apples and oranges and chocolate. They refilled their bottles in the clear, flowing water of the stream.

Argus grew restless and set off on some private mission along the water's edge. The man took no notice. He lay back on the grass to watch the high clouds of summer. The girl was thoughtful. She delved into her panniers and brought out a small washbag. She made him sit up at the edge of the stream and came to kneel behind him. She took scissors from the bag and began to cut off his long, matted hair.
He made no objection. The touch of the girl's hands on his neck was gentle and delicate beyond belief. It made his scalp tingle, then pump with blood. Pleasure exploded in his head. She cast the handfuls of hair into the stream as they came away. First she cut the length, then she began to fashion a design. She was concentrated entirely on her work, and it was this absorption more than anything which made the moment so sensual.

She moved onto trimming his beard. When the scissors would cut no closer, she lathered his chin with soap and continued with a razor. Her movements were as clean, confident and precise as his had been to repair the puncture.

As first his hair, then his beard was removed, he felt himself unmasked, exposed. The warmth of the sun on his cheek was exquisite. He crawled towards the stream on his front and immersed the whole of his head and neck underwater, rubbing to clean away the dirt and loose hair. He pulled back, gasping with the cold and the lack of air. He shook out his head like a dog, covering the girl with droplets of water.

Her childlike smile at the difference she had made was irresistible. He lent forward and kissed her lightly on the lips. Water ran off his face onto hers. Too soon she drew back.

'I will not be involved while this threat of violence hangs over you. Why can't you end this feud, or whatever it is?'
He looked at her. He knew he felt love, but it couldn't transcend his sordid predicament. For her and those like her, when pressure built up there was always the boundless world of imagination, into which violent thought would dissipate like heated water into an expansion vessel. For others, without imagination, violence would burst out of unvented systems.

He gave no answer, but the sadness in his eyes spoke of the compassion in his heart. She understood that there would be confrontation. She wanted no part of it.

They moved on. Argus had not returned. Secretly, the man feared losing him. His company illuminated the dim quarry life. Outwardly he maintained that the hound should be free to choose for himself.

The sensations on his neck, cheeks and chin were new and delicious. The sunlight, the moving air,the beads of liquid hanging from the skin. He felt the secrets of his soul racing to disport themselves on the contours of his face.

They cycled through one of the few high moorland villages. Invaded by summer tourists, abandoned to the isolation of winter. Fifty years of such alternation gave it a sinister, schizoid air.

The pattern changed as they approached the Moor's southern fringe. There were more farms, built long and low beneath generous quilts of thatch. The land was fenced in with intricate walls of granite. They admired the view south, which dropped away suddenly to a coastal plain and the sea. They headed back north, anxious to keep to the high ground.

By teatime, they had almost completed a loop of the moorland country. They stopped at a farmhouse advertising cream teas. He insisted on treating her. It was an authentic farmstead, with low granite lintels and mullioned windows. They stooped through the porch, and turned off the cross-passage into an immaculate parlour. Half a dozen tables with Windsor chairs lurched on uneven flagstones. One wall was an ancient oak screen, another a massive granite fireplace.

They exchanged conspiratorial grins. They were not alone. A large party occupied two tables. Both men and women wore thick socks inside heavy walking boots, with gaily coloured anoraks tied round their waists.

The lady of the house came to take orders. Through the kitchen door opposite they glimpsed a world of warm, blissful cosiness. An old cream Aga, a scrubbed pine table, various figures worshipping at the hearth. For an instant, the two outsiders coveted the domestic inclusion of that kitchen.

They shared a pot of tea and a round of scones. They accepted mutely the uncertainty which held them suspended in mid flight. Beginnings were good, and prolonged beginnings even better.

When they emerged from the farmhouse, they found Argus lying down where the two bicycles were propped together against a wall. His look was mildly resentful. The man pulled at his ears.
    'It's no good accusing me. You were the one who went off without us.'
Reunited. The adrenalin of the gang resuscitated their tired limbs. They stopped at the last viewpoint on the edge of the plateau. They could see north across Charrafin country as far as the redland. They were loth to plunge down from the enchanted high world. They were unwilling to break a spell which might never be recast. He lent across to kiss her still astride his bicycle, and lost his balance, bringing them both giggling to the ground. Argus barked at their mirth.

Eventually, there was nothing for it but to accept the dividend. They set off on the long descent, begrudging the kinetic energy which hummed off their tyres. For once, Argus lost his grace and was dishevelled in his efforts to keep up.

They were quiet with contemplation over the last few miles of hushed woodland. The steep, closed valleys pushed them back to introspection. He left the girl where they had met that morning, by the granite cross.

19.

A few mornings later, on his way down to the campsite, he noticed a van parked around the side of the village hall. Two workmen sat in the cab, eating sandwiches. A road gang probably, contracted to the council. When he cycled back up the hill at lunchtime, they were still there.

His stomach churned, his palms were damp. The waiting was taking away, so very slowly, his strength and his resolution. Instead of wheeling the bicycle into the quarry, he left it half-hidden near the road, making sure it could be seen from a passing vehicle. He doubled back down the hill. Calling Argus to his side, he followed the lane but kept in the fields, the other side of the hedge.

Halfway down, near a cross, he waited. It must have been ten minutes before he heard the growl of a diesel engine pulling up the hill. The van stopped at the junction. It was the same two men. They were talking about something, but the noise of the engine covered their voices.

After a while, they continued on up the hill. He raced back after them, keeping tight to the hedge. The van moved ahead, he couldn't match its speed uphill. His lungs were tight with pain, he must be there in time to see if they slowed or stopped by the entrance. He failed. When he reached the top, all he could hear was the relieved clatter of the engine coasting down the other side.

He swore. He was none the wiser. He might be paranoiac, seeing danger in a couple of council workmen travelling the lanes to clean out ditches and gulleys. Or they were close, watching and waiting. He sat under the awning in front of the cave and built up the fire. He tried to eat something but found that he had no appetite. He thought about gathering up his belongings and making a run for it. Now, while he still could. There was no shame in it. He was outnumbered, outgunned. Best to keep moving, keep them guessing.

Slowly, he calmed himself. If he ran now, he would be running for ever. He had a good position, he should make use of his advantage. He forced himself to go over the plan in his mind, again and again. He had a chance, with luck. First line of defence, the pit. Second line of defence, the olive green rope he had stretched across the mouth of the quarry at neck height. If two came together, he might be in trouble. But he gambled that one would be look-out and driver, the other the trained assailant.

He also guessed that they would come at night. It made sense to use the cover of darkness to hide their attack and their escape. They would try to catch him asleep. A single bullet, with silencer. Simple, clean job with least risk of interference or outside witness. And if they came at night, they would be sure to come one at a time. It would be too confusing otherwise. They might end up shooting each other, lost in a strange place in the dark.

He made certain he had several days' supply of firewood piled up next to him under the awning. Then he sat down to wait. To wait for death maybe. He shuddered, and cast the thought from his mind.

Instead, he focused on the life of the woodland around him. He watched his friends come to the bird table opposite. He loved the nut hatch, and the spotted woodpeckers best of all. He had taken to buying a few peanuts in a net for them. Their drum was insistent but friendly somehow, a neighbourly knock at the door. The call of the nut hatch during the day he found rather exotic. He could imagine himself in some foreign jungle.

At dusk, he sat quite still and was lost in the concert which came in surround sound from every woodland tree and bush. They sang goodnight, maybe goodbye. He liked it best when the climax was over and the diminuendo set in. He wondered if they could fall asleep as they sang, like the parent storyteller sometimes did. At the end, the strident alarm of the blackbird. He tried to guess which was the last call of all.

The night was calm and moonlit. Maybe they would favour that. Maybe they wouldn't. He saw shapes moving everywhere. He wanted to put on the headphones and listen to the radio, anything to distract his mind. But he didn't dare. He must remain alert, vigilant.

He kept his clothes on, and his boots. He propped his back against the rockface, and allowed himself to doze a little, sitting up. Argus sensed the tension. His ears were pricked and attentive. The man was overwhelmed with affection and gratitude. Without Argus he felt as if he couldn't survive the ordeal.

His vigil lasted until morning. At times he woke in a panic, not knowing how long he had been asleep. His reward was to hear the dawn chorus from the beginning, from the very first hesitant note. He showered in it, letting the music rinse away the terror of the night. He didn't know how many more such nights he could stand.

20.

He didn't leave the quarry. He stayed put and waited. He kept the fire going with wet logs and foliage mixed in with his dry firewood, so that the smoke would be seen from the village. He thought of himself as a brave, doing a war dance and sending smoke signals.

In the afternoon, it began to rain steadily. The day was still, without a ruffle of wind. The pop of the droplets falling on fresh summer foliage calmed him. Water began to penetrate the makeshift thatch of the awning. He considered putting on his waterproof clothing, but the air was mild, and the fire kept him warm. Besides, he didn't care to encourage a defensive mood.

Instead, he stripped down to his shorts and boots. He took a blackened branch from the fire and let it cool. Then he began to smear himself with its charcoal. All over his face, chest and legs. He went over to the spring and further covered his skin with the wet earth.

He tied the bowie-knife in its sheath to his waist. The broad roll of adhesive tape fitted over his wrist as a bracelet. He made sure his left hand could move faultlessly to turn on and off his head torch. He practiced clamping a bunch of cable ties between his teeth.

Argus observed his preparations with fond indulgence. Whatever was going on, it looked like an adventure. After the evening meal, the man grew restless. He had sat waiting long enough. He clipped the radio to his shorts and put on the headphones. He tuned in to some rhythmic music and danced around the fire. He sensed again the left over memory of other lifetimes. It felt so good to be stripped of easy resources and reduced to the bare necessities. He had his wits, his instinct and the fitness of his youth.

Later, his spirits tumbled back down from their euphoria. He didn't care what happened. He sunk into a fitful and troubled sleep, with his back propped against his rucksack, ready packed.

They came for him some time after midnight. It was Argus who saved him, awake and alert whilst the man slept off the madness of his lone war dance. Moonlight was diffused through a layer of cloud. The rain had stopped, and the hound's pricked ears detected far off their approach. His growl was long and low and charged with such terrible menace that the man was instantly conscious and clear-headed.

He reached out an arm to touch Argus' head. Thanks, but hush now. Take directions from me. Stay put for a while, until I call. Yes, I know, but please just stay there. Keep out of the way. Guard the hearth.

He scuttled forwards across the quarry floor on hands and knees. The motion brought on another vision. He was an ape man, and this was his jungle territory. He had an absurd desire to stand up and beat his chest. He swore at himself and demanded focus. Or he would soon be a dead ape.

He headed for the little hide he had prepared on the higher side of the trap. He must be there in position before any arrival, without making a noise. He had cleared a wide path of any twigs or obstacles during daylight, and had practised the manoeuvre several times to fix the coordinates in his head.

He crouched low when he reached there and listened. Nothing. Stay calm and wait. Breathe. He forced in great lungfuls, and tried to dilute the adrenalin. There was a mirror somewhere in his conscious which showed him as he was. A man dressed only in shorts and covered in soot and mud. The matted hair and wild beard now missing. Trying to ensnare a trained, armed assailant with the cobwebs of childhood imagination. It was absurd. Thankfully he was well past the point of no return. Doubt go mock yourself. I am beyond your reach. There was nothing else to do but listen and wait.

It can only have been a few minutes, but when two heartbeats instead of one inflate each second, the brain's turmoil may set down a lifetime's trauma. He would relive the waiting and the fear many times over. At last he heard signs of an approach, and in an instant his agony was drop-forged into cooling purpose.

Through a hole in the hide he could just make out the shape of someone moving forwards along the entrance track. The movements were slow and cautious, punctuated by moments of still attention. He had to remain in a squat to be under cover, but as his muscles tensed this became increasingly painful. He needed to move, even just to stretch out or stand up.

The figure on the track had come to a halt just a pace or two in front of the trap. It was very still and appeared to be listening or considering. Go on, go on just a bit further and you'll hear something, you damn fool. Like the crack of rotten wood. The concentration of will in his head leaked into his body, and he found himself pushing forward with his hands at the branches of the hide.

The figure began to move again. One step, two. The third, on the right foot, broke through the false roof of the pit with a crisp snap. The outline of the body, which had up until then been so calm and poised, suddenly burst out into a windmill of backward flailing arms. The weight had fallen onto the left leg, which tried to hold vertical. It was a moment out of time, of abstract fascination. The man watched his bid to survive played out in the contortions of a figure refusing to fall.

Then suddenly the trap pulled down its prey. The crunch of that right foot had taken the body beyond the critical point of balance. The left leg buckled, and with an explosion of dead wood the figure disappeared into the earth.

His torment continued. He had to hold back the urge to rush forwards immediately and throw himself upon his attacker. He had thought about it endlessly, and this was never the best plan. Sure enough, there were dark cursings, but in no time the top of a head appeared, and two arms thrust out with a pistol clamped between two hands. The arms swept through a full circle, and the gun jabbed at the darkness.

The attacker expected to be attacked. But no-one came. The figure was uneasy, still patrolling the air with the gun, but the movements were losing their conviction. There was only so long that an armed man could be comfortable standing in a hole in the ground in a strange wood. The figure moved to the front of the pit. The arms separated. The right hand held the gun. Then both hands were placed palms down on the edge above, and the body made a few experimental leaps upwards. Finally, with a determined surge, the figure rose from the earth, the feet scrabbled for purchase and the arms levered up until the elbows locked.

Now. This was the moment. His attacker was defenseless. With all the weight transferred to the hands, the gun was out of action. Impossible to move up and out quickly, madness to drop back down.

As the man burst from his hide, he clamped the cable ties between his teeth and reached with his left hand to illuminate the head torch. Two great strides down, and the beam of the torch picked out a face of astonished panic. The eyes closed in instinctive protection from the piercing halogen light. Perfect. A blinded assailant at his mercy.

His left boot smashed down on the right hand holding the gun, whilst the right boot accelerated through an arc of more than fifty degrees and landed with breathtaking force into the solar plexus. The figure exploded in bruised agony, the injured right hand lost its grip on the gun and the body fell back into the pit. The man jumped feet first after it, and both boots slammed down into the midriff from two metres above. He pulled the limp figure onto its front, and with one knee on the back of its neck he put the two hands together and pulled a cable tie tight around the wrists. Then he moved lower, and kneeling on the back of the calves he ratcheted another around the ankles.

He could feel that the figure was winded and trying desperately to breathe. He couldn't afford to let it cry out for help. With one knee in the small of the back, he jerked the head backwards by the hair and looped a thick band of adhesive tape over the mouth and round the back of the head, taking care to leave the nasal airway clear. Then he pulled the feet back to meet the hands, and linked the two cable ties with a third.
Nicely trussed. Tiredness threatened to envelop him. He wanted to sit, to relax, to feel relieved. Instead he used the figure as a step and launched himself out of the pit. No let up until the end and he was sure that out there somewhere was a second attacker.

21.

He switched off the headtorch as soon as he found the gun. He put a cable tie around the trigger guard and carried it by the tie rather than leave his finger prints on the barrel. He checked the rope across the quarry on his way back to the cave. No-one had tested its guillotine. Argus had disappeared from his lair.

He wrapped the gun in a plastic bag and hid it at the back of the cave. It was tempting to keep it on him just in case, but he soon dismissed the idea. Let it be a test of wits, and of fortune.

He went over to the spring to drink. Fear had dried him out. Adrenalin trembled away through his fingers. The shadow of langour stalked him. With his head under the little fountain coming out of the rock, water ran down his neck and over his face. He thought of the moment with the girl on the Moor. Of the droplets of water from the stream running off his face on to hers as he kissed her.

The hydrate of memory and cool liquid spread its vigour through his body. He had a reason, a motive to succeed. Something worth fighting for, since fight there must be. He moved quickly along the quarry wall, and back towards the road. He illuminated the pit for a few seconds to check that the figure tied up there was breathing normally. He listened for any movement, but heard none.

His way was out along the track. Slow and cautious. He tried to imagine what had happened to Argus, and wondered whether the next opponent would be armed. It seemed probable. He felt exposed, now that he was moving forward instead of lying in wait. His trap had brought initial success, but he realised that the remainder of his plan was nothing but a jumble of hope and uncertainty.

He covered the final distance to the gateway onto the road crawling on his belly. Almost there he heard footsteps on the tarmac. He rolled sideways into the long grass, and clamped his jaw tight around the bundle of cable ties when the stinging nettles welcomed him. They were worst around his arms, neck and face. Their burning distracted his fear.

A figure approached the gate. It was only a few metres away, but as long as he didn't move, his war paint would keep him camouflaged. The figure held a mobile phone, and was pressing urgently at the keypad. It could be trying to contact the other gunman, or perhaps it had panicked and was summoning help. Could there be others close by?

Suddenly, the figure swivelled back round to face the road, still and alert. It had seen or heard something there. It moved off the verge and exchanged the mobile phone for a gun. It took a few paces down the road. The man could no longer see what was going on. He rolled back on to the track, and used his elbows to move his head up to the gate.

Damn. Trotting up the road towards the figure was Argus. The man was powerless to help. He felt instantly very sick, and very angry. What the hell was the hound doing there in the road, and couldn't it sense the danger? He was condemned to watch Argus being shot, and then his fury would burn out of control. Everything was going wrong, slowly, right in front of him.

Yet there was something rather extraordinary about Argus' trot. He could have been out for a Sunday stroll. His manner suggested that all was well, and normal, and within rights, whereas in fact it was the middle of the night and he was approaching a very hostile stranger. The hound gave no hint of suspicion or aggression. Rather he behaved as if he knew the stranger well and quite expected him to be there. No growl, no barred teeth, just the usual dopey, gawky air he adopted amongst friends.

The man watched from behind the gate. He was fascinated. His jaw relaxed, and he nearly dropped the bundle of ties. The figure, too, was fascinated. It stood, legs slightly apart, in the middle of the road, with the right hand holding the gun pointed at Argus. But it did not fire. It could not fire in cold blood on a friendly dog that approached in casual greeting. It was flattered by the assumption of intimacy.

Argus trotted right up to the figure. He stopped in front of it. He put his head between the stranger's legs in the usual nuzzle of greeting. And then he added a variation. He opened his jaw, and with a swiftness, and a purpose, and a ferocity which were breathtaking he bit the stranger's genitals. He bit very hard and he didn't let go.

The fabric of the trousers offered minimal protection. The hound's pointed teeth ripped through the cotton and the buttoned fly, and sunk into the flesh beneath. The pain was conveyed so quickly that there was no time for surprise. Or even reprisal. The figure's mouth opened in a great howl of agony. His hands came together by instinct, to clasp protectively at the body parts under attack. The gun in his right hand caught Argus a heavy blow on the jaw. As it did so, it went off. Perhaps by design, perhaps by accident.

The man heard the fizz of the bullet passing through a silencer. He heard Argus yelp. He saw the hound scrabble sideways back towards the quarry. He imagined the worst. Fury detonated in his head. Its incandescence blocked rational thought. Its energy carried him up and over the gate and towards the figure bent double in the road. He was approaching fast from behind. The figure began to straighten up. He kicked out hard, below the buttocks. He didn't think about it, it just happened that way. He kicked harder than he had a few minutes earlier, at the first attacker. He kicked in frustration at the madness of it all. He kicked to avenge his friend.

His boot caught the injured genitals. That brought on a howl even greater than before. Momentum carried the boot on, into collision with the hands. The gun was sent clattering away down the road. The last of the followthrough brought his shin up against the buttocks. The force was sufficient to pitch the figure head first onto the tarmac.

The success of this single blow shocked him into thought. His left hand switched on the head torch as he sunk to his knees. His left knee clamped the figure's neck, his right landed between the shoulder blades. He struggled for a while before he managed to loop a cable tie around the wrists. The legs were still flailing wildly. He pulled the body onto its side to land a stun punch into the solar plexus. That gave him enough of an advantage to tie the ankles, and finally to truss hands and feet together as before.

He sat on the tarmac, dazed and drained. The figure began to shout abuse at him. He taped up its mouth. He sat for a long time, shaking violently and unable to move. He felt no elation. Not even relief. The experience left him numb in mind and body.

22.

He became aware that he was very cold. He dragged the body off the road, through the gate into the wood and cable-tied it to a small tree. He recovered the gun from the road and made his way back towards the quarry with it.

He dreaded finding Argus. Crawled off into some corner to die. They were a team now. He didn't know if he had it in him to carry on alone.

Back at the cave there was no sign of him. He built up the fire and sat under the awning to feed the flames. He was on the verge of catalepsy. Only the fire held him back. Its dancing light bound him to life. Gradually the roaring warmth found its way across into his body. He began to revive.

Soon he was hungry. A good sign. He ate some fruit, and biscuits. He put on a large pan of water to heat, and then started to wash the war off his skin. It had dried on and was hard to shift. He sponged on soap and warm water, and began to feel clean again. He dressed and drank some tea. His world began to revolve once more.

Time to take stock. There were two men, bound and gagged, and now his responsibility. A hound somewhere in the wood, probably dead or bleeding to death. Make a plan from that.

It was unbearable to think of Argus. Instead he considered his two attackers. He felt sure there were only two, because any others would have come by now. How had they got there? He had seen no car or van in the road, but then they would not have wanted to park in such an obvious way. Somewhere there must be a vehicle. And if he found the keys, he could use it himself.

Supposing he got hold of the keys, what then? There was no point in going to the police. His criminal record spoke for itself, and even if they took him seriously the worst charge for which he held proof would be a firearms offence. Besides, it solved nothing. They would just come for him again, or others in their place.

To stay afloat for seven years in prison, he had needed a life-buoy. He had pushed it down beneath the water and kept it there, with all his weight upon it, and never let it back up. For as long as he couldn't see it, he didn't have to know that he was in danger of drowning without it.

There beneath the surface it had remained ever since. Now, as he sat by the fire, still in shock and traumatised by the events of the night, the life-buoy slipped from under him and rose to the surface. It was a revelation. From the moment that the judge had passed sentence, he had never dared to look upon the truth of what had happened, and why he was in prison. And now, there it was again, floating before him. A love, greater than himself, which he yearned to give once more.

Suddenly it was obvious what he had to do. The girl was right. It was time to end this misguided feud. A plan formed in his head. A destination. He felt all the better for it.

He took the disposable camera over to the pit. He dropped down into it, and searched through the gunman's pockets. No keys, but he found a mobile phone and a wallet. He didn't look in the wallet, for he didn't want to know anything about his assailant. But he kept the phone. He sat the figure facing up in a corner, and took a couple of flash photographs. He moved to the second prisoner and repeated the process. This time he also found a bunch of keys.

He set off down the road to look for their vehicle. He didn't believe they would have wanted to leave it too far away. The junction where he had seen a van stop a few days back was really a crossroads. The fourth road was an old green lane, and a dead end. He followed it round a corner and came across a white panelled van parked in a gateway.

One of the keys fitted. He imagined the van had probably been stolen, although in that case it was strange to find a key. Inside there was nothing much. Some maps. The remains of a meal. A holdall which he left untouched.

He drove up the hill, and reversed the van into the quarry entrance. He loaded his bicycle towards the front and then untied the figure from the tree and dragged it over to the back of the van. He half heaved, half rolled it in.
He made his way back to the cave. The camera, the guns and both phones he put into a plastic bag and hid them in a fissure in the roof of the cave. He gathered up what possessions he hadn't yet packed and made a bundle of them.

It was time to look for Argus, and then leave his quarry home. He had no wish to do either. He piled the last of his firewood onto the flames for a farewell bonfire. The light began to reach across to the rockface opposite. It was a ghostly, dancing cinema.

He was standing there, enjoying his final moments of freedom, when a forlorn figure made a second, limping approach to his fire. Argus.

Down but not out. There was no mistaking him, even in the half light of the flames. He wanted to rush over to the hound, but stopped himself. There were certain things you did unaided, including getting home after an eventful night.

He watched the hound move painfully towards the cave. Maybe it was fanciful of him, but he thought that Argus' bearing spoke clearly enough: I shall manage by myself. Once he had reached his lair, the hound collapsed onto his right side and lay breathing heavily.

The man dropped down on his knees beside his friend. He used the head torch to examine the wounds. The left jaw was swollen and bleeding where the gun had caught it. And the left shoulder had a channel of flesh missing, where the bullet must have grazed through. The hound had lost a lot of blood, and was very weak. But otherwise not so badly injured.

He felt tears of relief and gratitude flood into his eyes. He stroked the hound's head and ears, and marvelled at his loyalty. They were in it together, Argus had made that much clear.

He fetched water in a bowl, and then left him lying by the fire. He had the problem of how to get his first prisoner out of the pit. He took down the rope which he had tied across the quarry and threw it over the branch nearest to the trap. He tied one end around his prisoner, and pulled on the other. It took some time, and the effort warmed him right through, but finally he succeeded in hauling the body up and onto the rim. He dragged it over to the van and loaded it alongside the other one, then returned for his belongings.

He put some clothes in the passenger footwell to make a nest. He carried Argus wrapped in his coat and laid him carefully in the van.

He went back one more time into the quarry. He had made his farewells. Looking across at the embers of his bonfire and the makeshift awning over the cave, he knew that never again would he feel so free as he had done there.

23.

Time no longer counted as he drove up the track to the girl's cottage. It was three, maybe four o'clock in the morning, but so what.

He had blindfolded his prisoners to be sure they would see nothing, and tied them both to opposite sides of the van so that they couldn't help each other.

The headlights picked out the motley face of the buildings. He left the engine running for a while, hoping to wake her. A light came on upstairs, then after a few minutes there was more light downstairs and the front door opened far enough to show the girl's bleary, confused face. He moved forward into her view, and she opened the door wider to invite him in.

Neither spoke. He sat at the table, and she put the kettle to heat on a gas burner. She came to sit opposite him. His look was drained, but resolute. Hers was questioning, even slightly amused. Confident rather than apprehensive.

'Argus is in the van. He's hurt, but not too badly. Very weak from blood loss. Can I bring him in?'
She nodded, but didn't really take it in. The man came back carrying Argus in a coat. He laid him on the table.

Her brain began to function. She sought out an enamel bowl, swabs, antiseptic and dressings. The first hot water went into the bowl, and more was put on to make tea. The man held Argus gently whilst she cleaned the wounds with care. There were no words, only the hound's whimperings. He studied her face, but she avoided his gaze and concentrated on her work. She put a dressing on the shoulder, but the jaw was more difficult and she decided in the end to leave it open. The hound's own saliva should prevent infection.

He settled Argus on an old sofa and covered him for warmth. He sat opposite the girl at the table to drink tea and munch biscuits. Now she held his gaze, and encouraged an explanation. He couldn't decide how much to say.

'It sounds pathetic, I know, but right now you and Argus are my only friends. He has saved my life, and paid dearly for it. I have come to ask your help. Three favours in fact. But you can see the violence I am caught up in, and I will think no less of you if you send me away instead.'

She considered this, whilst her eyes still shone with a mixture of amusement and sorrow. Although there was no reply, he could feel her urge him to go on.

'You were right before. It is time to settle the quarrel. I have decided to see it through, straightaway, whatever the cost. Two men came to kill me tonight. They are in the back of their van out there, tied up but unharmed. I must take them back to the person who sent them.'

He paused, and waited for her reaction, her questioning. She remained silent, but nothing in her turned away from him.

'The first favour concerns Argus. He is too weak to travel, and needs nursing. Would you keep him here with you?'

She nodded, without hesitation. Tears had begun to form in her eyes, but the man felt calm and still held her gaze.

'The second concerns the old man at the campsite. I cannot let him down after the trust he has shown me. Today I would normally turn up there at around ten to clean the service block and mow the grass. Can you do this for me until I return? Hopefully in a few days time.'

She thought for a bit, wondering whether she would be able to manage the antique lawnmowers she had seen at work there. But the owner would explain how everything worked, and again she nodded her agreement.

'And perhaps you should warn him that I may not return at all. The third favour is for me. I have hidden a plastic bag in a crack in the roof of the cave, up at the quarry. The old man knows the spot. In that bag are the mobile phones and guns belonging to the men who tried to kill me, as well as a camera containing photographs of them. If you do not hear from me again, say within 48 hours, I would like that bag to find its way to the police. If I return, I will deal with it myself, as well as the pit I have left open at the quarry.'

Her tears began to flow. They trickled down to the summit of her cheeks, and paused there, before accelerating on to her lips and chin. Her eyes held his in silent, sad entreaty. Make sure you return. Do not leave me with this task.

Looking into such eyes, his composure left him. The life-buoy no longer held him afloat, but bobbed out of reach. One ancient love had been rekindled in him, and now a new one was about to overwhelm him. To send him across the table for solace after seven barren years. He wanted to hold her, to hug her, to kiss away her tears. To lie with her upstairs and never feel the need to leave. To wake in the night and sense her warmth and her quiet breath beside him.

He felt his will collapsing. He wanted to love, and be loved. He pushed backwards on the chair and stumbled out the door without a word. Please, no more goodbyes.

24.

He raced his way across country along the lanes, following the route he had travelled first on foot when he arrived from prison. The roads were empty, even when he reached the City. He had a view of it lit up below him from the top of the last hill. For once peaceful, serene, almost entirely in bed. He loved the loneliness of driving on empty roads at darkest night. For as long as he kept moving, his isolation would not putrefy into despair.

The fuel gauge showed nearly full. They had had the foresight to fill up for their escape. He allowed himself a smile at that. He stopped at the services where he joined the motorway and drank strong black coffee. It was something he never touched, and he knew it would keep him awake and alert for hours to come. The two prisoners had their blindfolds and gags removed. He promised to replace them immediately if either one spoke or made trouble. He headed north, and watched the dawn break to his right. There was something exciting, satisfying even, in his mission. It might end in death, but he no longer feared that. Whatever happened, it would serve as a resolution to seven years' waiting. And for more people than just himself. He anticipated the coming confrontation in his mind, and explored the possible outcomes.

The van was a recent model. It covered the distance with ease and comfort. When he was happy with his mental preparation, he switched on the radio to help himself relax. The mix of news, weather, and music did not hold his attention, but was strangely soothing in the background. He pretended for a while that he was a tradesman on his way to a job, as others might see him. It was reassuring to construct a cocoon of pretence, and inhabit it playfully. Part of him envied his make-believe self.

After an hour they crossed over a broad river mouth by the sea, and skirted another City. Here there was more traffic, but it was still too early for rush hour volumes. At the interchange he swapped motorways and headed east towards the Capital.

Now there were lorries on the move, and some cars overtaking very fast. He switched off the radio in order to concentrate. It was a long time since he had driven anywhere, let alone through the thrust of motorway traffic in a strange vehicle. With the rear view mirror he kept an eye on his passengers. They preferred to maintain their silence, rather than be gagged and blindfolded again.

The early rush had begun by the time he reached the suburbs. He had a moment of panic trying to find his route. Everything seemed unfamiliar at first, until he calmed himself and started to recognise a few landmarks. He turned off the motorway and made his way south into an area of apparent wealth and prosperity.

From now on he was guessing. He knew the name of the house and the type of property to expect, but he had never been there or seen pictures. It was too risky to seek directions from a passer-by. As a last resort, he could park somewhere and ask in a shop, but that would definitely mean replacing the gags. He drove up and down the tree-lined avenues for a while, looking left and right. There was only so long he could do that, without attracting attention. The sweat forming under his arms and on his forehead alarmed him. This would never work if he showed himself fearful and desperate.

He decided to change his plan. Driving around was proving too stressful. He looked instead for somewhere quiet but unremarkable to park the van. There was a spot near the Green which looked suitable. Somewhere you might leave your car when walking a dog. He pulled off the road, and jumped in the back quickly to tape up his prisoners' mouths and tie them still. The second one began to shout when he saw what was happening, but there was no-one close enough to hear.

He transferred the contents of his rucksack into the bike's panniers. His money and papers he kept in his pocket. He hesitated for a while over the bowie-knife, but held to his resolve to be unarmed. When it was safe, he opened the van doors and handed out the bicycle, leaning it against the side panel. Inside again, he covered over the rear window so that no-one could see the two men tied up on the floor.

He locked the van and set off to find his destination by bicycle. In no time his mood changed. The stress was gone, the pressure was off. He could enjoy his surroundings, and his mission. Only the bicycle could do this for him. It defied the weight on his shoulders, pinning him down. However low his spirits, it rejuvenated them and set him rolling, joyful and free.

Now that he had time to look about, he soon found the house. It was a mock Tudor mansion, set well back from the road, and surrounded by a high brick wall. The entrance gates were automated. Beside them an intercom was set into the pillar, with a plate bearing the name he recognised. He had decided his approach would be straightforward, head-on. No skulking, no shame. It was still too early for any sign of life outside in the garden. He pressed on the buzzer.

25.

There was no reply. He sensed a cruel absurdity. All this way, with such anticipation, and there would be no-one at home. Everyone away, on holiday. No, it wasn't possible. They would be following the success of a long-awaited act of justice. He pressed again, longer this time. There was a camera angled down from atop the pillar. He looked directly into the lens.

The intercom speaker hummed alive. There was no word, no greeting at all. He continued to stare at the camera and speak.
　　'I have two prisoners. They are unharmed. I want to exchange them for 5 minutes of your time. I am not carrying a weapon.'
He opened his coat towards the camera, lifted his shirt, scrunched his pockets. The speaker clicked off.

Nothing happened. He began to feel rather a fool, standing behind the gates. They would hardly kill him there, in front of their own home. Maybe they would just ignore him. He continued to stand, staring with cool resolution at the camera.

Eventually he heard the front door open. From the porch emerged a tall, silver-haired figure dressed impeccably in corduroy and tweed. A few paces out, standing on raked gravel, it stopped and faced him. Even at that distance, the information his brain gathered within a few seconds was more or less complete. The clothes, the posture, the bearing, the stance. They spoke of wealth and privilege, health and pride. But the material and body tissue served only to enclose a void. The inside was hollowed out and empty. Dessicated by grief.

The figure moved towards him at the gates. It was poised and graceful in its motion, even late in life. But the eyes soon caught his attention. They were so terribly pained and sad. Flecked with anger. The eyes of someone cheated by life. Somehow out-manoeuvred by it, and left as a bystander. Resentful, not resigned.

The two men faced each other through the elaborate filigree of the entrance gates. Their eyes locked on in such earnest, but neither man flinched or blinked. The encounter was not so much aggressive and hostile, as deeply probing.

'This time I got lucky, I survived. But I know your resources are greater than mine. If you want me dead, in the end you will succeed.'

It was the first direct exchange. He remembered looking across from the dock to the witness box, and seeing a younger face, still full of hate.

'There is something you deserve to know, and you should hear it from me. I did not kill your son. I confessed to the police. I had the perfect motive. I pleaded guilty in court. But I did not kill your son.'

He stopped and waited for a reaction. A cry of outrage or of pain. A hiss of menace. A gunshot. Nothing. No word, no change in countenance. The figure was present, but refused to acknowledge its presence.

'Only one person knows what happened that night at the flat. The person who killed your son. You should know the truth, but it is not for me to try and tell it. The person who did it must be allowed to explain.'

The father's face betrayed a sudden look of tired hopelessness. The sandy foundations of his revenge were already giving way.

'When you know the full story, you will understand why I lied. You may not forgive me, but I know you will understand. Wait until you know the truth before you kill me, if you must. I am the only person who can send your son's killer to you. And that is exactly what I intend to do.'

The two men continued to face each other through the ironwork gates. On one side an imperceptible frown of doubt, on the other confessional relief. Something of the charge that existed between them had leaked into the earth, and fused their feet into stillness.

'Before the end of the year, someone else will ring here like me and confess to you. You will not hesitate to believe their story. This is my promise. It is the most I can do to set things right, and make amends. There is no ruse. If I try to deceive you, all I gain is a life on the run, looking over my shoulder, and I have that already.'

He leaned forward and carefully posted the bunch of keys through the letter box.

'If, when you know the truth, you are still thirsty, come yourself next time. This is between us, noone else. You will find the men in their van, not far from here, but far enough in case they have ideas of their own when they are released. I have kept back their phones and guns as insurance, for the time being.'

There was no more to say. He turned and took a step towards the bicycle leant against the wall. Then he stopped , and swivelled back to face his adversary.

'I have lost seven years of my life because of what happened that night, and I wasn't even involved. But believe me when I say that my loss is slight compared to yours. From one father to another, that much I do know.'

26.

He headed west. First towards the river, where he knew there was a traffic-free cycle path out of the Capital. The initial excitement of weaving his way through the cars and lorries soon diminished and he was grateful to find a pathway with a smooth surface devoted only to walkers and cyclists. It was a relief to be sheltered from the frantic engines and their foul, suffocating smoke trails.

He followed the great river upstream in a series of slow wimples through a flood plain. Developments squeezed the water from both sides, now commercial, now residential through a relay of satellite towns. He was used to the rigours of the hill country, where he had cycled for the past months. By comparison, the terrain was flat, and easy on the legs. The day was warm and still, and he had hopes of covering a good distance by nightfall, if he didn't fall asleep first. The effects of the caffeine were wearing off. He must be careful not to cycle off into the river's hungry flow.

He had been travelling mostly south-west, with the sun warming his left side. After a few hours, he felt it on the back of his neck, and knew he had turned to cycle north-west. The cycle path abandoned the river. There were short sections of road work, which made the traffic-free parts all the more delicious. The conurbation gave way to countryside, and stretches of cool woodland.

Around midday he arrived in a great Park. He slowed to take in the wonders of the landscape and the vistas towards a massive castle. In the town he bought bottled water and some food to make a picnic. Rice and beans from a delicatessen, fruit, biscuits, chocolate and cereal bars to keep him going later on. He sat with his back against one of the huge oaks and ate a lot. Then he remembered feeling a great tiredness closing him down.

He awoke in a panic. He looked for the sun and guessed it was mid-afternoon. That didn't seem so bad, and his bicycle was still there, leant against the tree trunk, and his pockets had not been disturbed. He set off again towards the west, more or less following in reverse the route he had driven up that morning. There were more built-up areas to negotiate, and some sections of busy road. This was the most stressful part of the journey, he told himself. Tomorrow he might relax and enjoy things more. Although the cycling was easy enough on the flat, his legs were used to the rhythm of ascent and descent. He had difficulties adapting to the monotony of steady pedalling. His temperament was better suited to the challenge of the hills and the reward of childish, helter-skelter downhill.

There was no question of paying for accommodation, he husbanded his savings too well to allow that. It was warm and dry enough to sleep rough, which he did in his bivi-bag hidden in a small wood.

By mid-morning on the second day it came to him that he was content. Almost entirely so. The last of the urban sprawl was behind him. He was travelling along the tow path of a beautifully engineered canal. He had begun to release himself at last from the guilt and pretence of seven years, even if a resolution was still a long way off. And he had a destination. Not so much a geographical destination, as an emotional one. He felt his love for the girl growing inside him, and dared to hope that it would be returned.

As long as the bicycle wheels purred over the tarmac of the pathway. As long as he felt the warm sunshine and soft breezes massage his skin. As long as the speed of his travel outpaced the sordid and mundane, making room for his ecstasy. For just so long would he continue to enjoy his contentment unalloyed.
He loved the canal. He was absorbed by its miniature world, by the comings and goings of its inhabitants. The grace of the heron, the panic of the moorhen. The trees and bushes of its avenue held songbirds in abundance. The stasis of its water was restful after the turbulence of the great river, and seemed to make a better foil for his own motion.

He thought again how perfect was the way a bicycle sliced through life. He greeted the morning dog walkers, saw a snapshot of their lives projected onto their faces and guessed at the nature of their homes from the manner of their pooches. Yet the glimpse came and went, soon to be replaced by another, giving him the rich beginnings of a hundred different stories, as well as the room to invent and imagine and leave so many questions unanswered. Only the bicycle could do this. Any form of engine or bodywork set up a barrier or exploded the magic of chance. The walk was just too slow and earthbound for elation and elevation. His boyhood kites never flew without a certain windspeed.

He marvelled at the variety and autonomy of the canal boats. Tiny gardens and terraces on deck. Their chimney flues spoke of cosy stoves within, their names on the bow of homely adventure. Dense wood was sheeny with varnish or garish with colour. It was still a little early in the season for busy water traffic, and most boats were tied up along the bank awaiting their summer parade. He came across a few under power, or negotiating the patient vigil of the lock gates.

Where houses had been built close to the canal, their gardens joined and exploited the waterway with ingenuity, or shut it out with mouldy fencing. It reminded him of travelling on the railway, which looks on the back of human industry, rarely seeing its facade.

If anything detracted from his contentment, it was the absence of a friend to share his joy. He missed Argus. The thought brought him to a skiddy halt. He hadn't yet telephoned the girl. He went in search of a phonebox.

27.

The middle section of the canal towpath remained a muddy track, overgrown in places and only suitable on foot. He followed the cycle route back onto country roads, and swapped the intimate world of the waterway for the vast skies and fields of the chalk downs. The contrast was refreshing, the hills invigourating. He rested for a couple of hours like the previous day. Sitting under a stand of beech trees, he surveyed the obsessive linear symmetry of arable fields, grooved into curvaceous chalk land.

He rejoined the towpath by a spectacular flight of locks, and watched spellbound from the garden of a tearoom as the narrowboats stepped their way up or down the steep incline. It was a toytown of three-dimensional activity in a two-dimensional world. It set his head to spin, and finally to ache.

By late evening the towpath ran out. The canal joined the river and he joined a disused railway track. By nightfall he was in the centre of the City which he had skirted nearly two days before, by way of the motorway interchange. He decided to take a train home from there, rather than attempt another long day's cycle. His body ached, his bicycle had begun to squeal loudly and if he caught the first train in the morning he could be at the campsite by ten and so save the girl a second tour of duty.

He slept on a bench, with his hands thrust protectively in his pockets and his bike cable-tied to his belt. He was so exhausted, he even slept well.

The morning train was full of clean-shaven, suited commuters. He stood out somewhat with his battered khakis, three-day stubble and whiff of exertion. In two days he had tried four of the ways of travelling on land, and he knew which he preferred, given the time. Even so, it was quite fun to travel at speed and at mercy. He had no say in the nature of his journey for as long as he stayed on the train. Such an escape from responsibility was a treat.

He got off at the City where months before he had got out of jail. From a phonebox on the platform he called the girl and promised to be at the campsite himself by ten.

He felt relieved. As he cycled west along the now familiar lanes, he compared his mood and his situation with those of his foot journey along the same route. Only with hindsight did he understand the fatigue and the fear and the deceit of his previous position. It was not over, but whatever happened now he felt he had removed the brand.

At the campsite he was greeted as ever by the old man's gentle good humour. He wondered how much the girl had told him, but his employer gave no indication of curiosity or judgement. The good weather had encouraged more campers to venture out in search of summer. He set to work cleaning, tidying and mowing. He was pleased to be busy. It camouflaged the awkwardness he felt about his trip away, and gave him the chance to regain the rhythm of his life around the village.

When he finished work about lunchtime, there was no-one else in the service block. He had the chance to shower, shave and wash his clothes. He pegged them out on the line and sat under the oak tree to think. Instead he fell asleep. His body was still making up for the lost night.

Later in the afternoon he woke and wondered where he would spend the night. A part of him had said goodbye to the quarry, never expecting to see it again. Did he really want to resume his secluded vigil there? He acknowledged that it would be a backward step. No need to decide yet. He packed everything into his panniers, and felt pleasure at the condensed simplicity of living off a bicycle. He set out to visit Argus and the girl.

There was time enough to grow nervous as he made his way past fond landmarks. The shop where they met so clumsily, the spot where they first saw each other, the gateway where he mended her puncture. It came to him slowly. No wonder he was apprehensive. In the past few days so much had changed. He had hidden behind the stigma of his brand. He had used his predicament as an excuse for detached isolation. This was no longer possible. It was time to go forward, one hand held out, as never before.

28.

The welcome Argus gave him, he might have been returning from an epic journey lasting nineteen years. The hound wagged and nuzzled, whimpered and barked. His jaw had healed well, and apparently his appetite had begun to return. But the shoulder injury was still sore, and he had resumed a three-legged limp.

The man sat on the bench in front of the cottage, and the girl brought him something to eat. He was suddenly very hungry, and felt embarrassed at how often this was the case in other people's houses. A coincidence, or a sign of meanness? Perhaps hunger was stimulated by the inhabitual.

What with Argus' greetings, they had avoided the need to face each other, and consider their nakedness. Reticent people needed their pets to speak for them. As he sat in the sun to eat, his naturalism returned. The energy there was so strong. When you were outside, you synchronised with its timeless pulse.

For the first time there was a bolster of explanation between them. The girl had never sought to know more than she was told. Now he knew he should volunteer his account. His stomach was full. The warmth of the sun and of his welcome relaxed him. He sensed quick indulgence at the thought of sharing his story.

'I have a daughter. She was just four when I last saw her. I can't imagine her as she must be now, at eleven. In prison, I taught myself not to think of her. It was my survival strategy. It would have destroyed me, to be aware of her growing up without me.'

He glanced sideways at the girl. She looked pale. He waited for her to make a movement, or begin to speak. She remained very still, her eyes lowered.

'We called her Judy. I had been sharing a house with her mother. First, as friends. Then, as lovers. The pregnancy was a surprise, but we both welcomed it. Afterwards, the problems began. She was too young really to lose her youth and freedom, just like that. Too weak to suffer the consequences. Our relationship fell apart, full of recrimination. We continued to live together for money reasons, and for convenience. As well as for Judy's sake. But we led separate lives. Strange to say, we became friends again.'

'How old were you?'

'We were the same age. We'd met at University. Eleven years back, so we must have been twenty-five. The adult world to explore. Good salaries coming in. The possibilities were boundless, which was more than half the trouble. She took the allotted pregnancy leave, then returned to her job. Fortunately, I was able to work mostly from home. When I had to be away, we used a childminder to cover any daytime absence.'

'What was your work?'

'I had trained as an architect. The arrangements worked alright to begin with, but then I noticed that she was disintegrating. I don't know why. Maybe guilt at not being a full-time mother to Judy, maybe lost in the middle, neither tied down nor free. She fell in with a strange crowd of socialites, involved in drugs. I was helpless to change or influence any of this. If I said something against, she was driven more towards.'

'Did it affect her relationship with Judy?'

'Not really. At least I couldn't see that it did. When she was with her, she was full of love and care. Not in a forced or dutiful way. The mother in her was still the same person I had known and loved. But there was a fault line in her character, and it was opening up under pressure. I knew she was having a fling with a man from a rich world. The son of an entrepreneur, with time and money on his hands.

Then one night I had a telephone call. Too awful to describe. I knew it was her, but she wasn't making any sense. Screaming and sobbing. She calmed down long enough to tell me where she was. I put Judy in the car and drove there. It was a house in a wealthy district, which belonged to the entrepreneur and had been used by them for their lovemaking.'

'Why go? You said your lives were separate. You had Judy to think of, too. If there was some problem she had made for herself, why not let her solve it?'

'I find it difficult to answer that. I think I always felt a strength in myself which corresponded to her weakness. Perhaps I wanted her to fall spectacularly, so that I could show my own reserves. I certainly wasn't prepared for what I found. The boyfriend was on the bed with a kitchen knife in his chest. The autopsy showed that he'd been on a serious trip. I guess so had she, though maybe to a lesser extent. She was becoming lucid. She kept saying that she had tried to end it.'

'End his life? End their affair?'

'I don't know. At the time I gave it little thought. It seemed clear to me that, whatever had happened, she was responsible for the knife and that she would go to prison for it. I felt certain that even a few years locked away would destroy her. I didn't dare to think how Judy would suffer for it. Deprived of her mother at four, followed by a lifetime's instability. I couldn't bear it. Maybe too there was a part of me which was enjoying being able to cope, being able to stay cool and to manage things. I don't think I followed through the logic of my own plan to where it would lead.

I sobered her up with coffee. Then I hit her several times. Gave her two black eyes and some proper bruising. It had to be convincing, and it brought her back to earth. I told her to take the car home with Judy and park it away from the house. To slip in the back quietly, get Judy settled and then ring the police. To say that she was worried. That I'd come home drunk, beaten the address of her lover out of her, then gone out. And not come back. I told her to stick to her story whatever, or we'd all suffer the more.'

'Was she really in a fit state to drive home and carry that off? I can't imagine how.'

'I think by this time she had begun to understand her situation. She took my lifeline without hesitation. I went round the house checking there was no trace of her from that evening. I found a bottle of whisky and forced myself to drink it. I made sure my prints were all over the knife handle. It didn't matter that hers were too, because she would have used it in the kitchen at any time. I got my story word perfect. Then I sat down to wait.'

29.

'You're telling me that all the time you were in prison, she never came to see you or brought Judy to visit her father?'

'It didn't surprise me. In many ways I was glad. It made it easier to survive, to pretend that they hadn't existed. To see Judy and not be able to be with her would have been far worse. I think she knew me well enough to figure that out. In any case, I had guessed she would disappear after the trial. She was an instinctive runaway. A bolter.'

The girl considered for a while. She was carefully fitting the pieces together.

'And the men who came to the quarry. They were sent by the father, by the entrepreneur?'

'Yes. He tried first in prison. There was a contract out on me. Maim or kill. But I made sure to get protection from some rich and powerful prisoners. I had kudos already. I had had the balls to murder a rival, to fight for my woman. I played that up, and flattered their egos by drawing elaborate plans for villas in Spain or mansions in the home counties. It got me through. I knew someone would try again after my release. Which is why I came to the quarry, to give myself a chance.'

He told the girl about his trip in the van to return the two men and confront the entrepreneur.

'I didn't tell him the full story. Just that I wasn't his son's killer, and that I promised to send the real killer to him. I don't want him looking for Judy and her mother before I do. He may guess, but I doubt it. In any case, I think the energy and hate have turned to dust inside him.'

'You mean to look for Judy? Or do you know where she is already?'

'No. I have no idea where they are. I have heard nothing for nearly seven years. But I can guess where to start looking. When Judy was on the way, we travelled in France, and were happy there. Her mother speaks good French, and I know she had friends in the South because we visited them once.'

'Have I got this right? You have no car, little money for travelling, but you are intending to set out to find your daughter, who might be anywhere in the world. With nothing more than a bicycle you got off the dump?'

'Well, yes. What choice do I have? I can't afford to wait. Now that I've allowed myself to consider the possibility, I couldn't wait even if I had to. I shan't be able to settle now, until I'm on the trail.'

'And me? How about me? You keep careering in and out of my life in rather dramatic fashion. How would you suggest I settle?' It was the first time he had heard her speak with an edge of reproach. It had the desired effect. He scrabbled frantically to emerge from the narrow rut of his life in crisis, and look about. He had been making assumptions and he'd better just own up.

'Yes, I am being selfish, but when people try to kill you, it does that to you. I have been assuming that you would come with me. Forgive me for that.'

The girl laughed. It seemed to him the first time he had heard her laugh so freely. He was trying to work out what it meant, which, in the circumstances, was not clear. She was mysterious. He plunged on.

'You leave me hanging. In my clumsy way I am asking you to come along. And you are laughing at me. Is that a yes or a no?'

'Neither. The idea is ridiculous. It's mad enough you disappearing off into the world on a search with no address. Now you want me to abandon my home and come as well. You're too much.

'Why don't you go up to the quarry? Do something sensible with those guns, before they get into the wrong hands. And fill in that pit of yours. The old man told me he went up there to see what was going on and nearly fell in it himself. He was very tickled to hear you actually caught someone with it. It made his day, if I hadn't already made it by flying around on that damned mower out of control. Come back tonight, and we'll have supper here.'

She was wonderful. Practical, calm and good-humoured. Sure of herself. He cycled very slowly along by the river, in a muse of love. Slowly, because the double act was back on the road. Argus would not be left behind, his ears flapping with every awkward bound.

He sought out the old man in his office, and asked sheepishly for the loan of a wheel barrow, and a shovel. The old man's grin was as broad as a letterbox. He left the bicycle down at the campsite, and wheeled the barrow up the hill, with Argus sat imperiously inside it.

It was strange to return to the quarry. Only a few days had passed since the terror of his night vigil there, and already it felt part of another life. He set to work, picking up the loose soil he had dumped in the trees down below the pit and tipping it back where it came from. He rescued the plastic bag from the roof of the cave and put it in a tupperware container he had used to carry food. He buried it about a metre down, where it wouldn't be found accidentally, but could still be retrieved. He began to marvel rather at his own ingenuity, until he remembered how luck had made all the difference on the night. Just the work of chance then, or was there the dividend of courageous adventure? He knew he didn't believe that either. He didn't wish to own up to what he really thought, even to himself. Which was that his brother had been there all along, to help. Just like 30 years before.

30.

He stayed the night.

At first, it was need which entwined itself around them. They shared its traces. The need to be held, to be loved, then to be released at last from the stifling tendrils of need's embrace. To see again, anew. Not just the foreground, but the setting too. The whole enticing panorama.

Which led them on to hold this time. To love at their own behest. The shared warmth. The union of smells. She smelt of cedarwood shingles, steaming in sunlight after rain. Of the barn with its leaky old lorry and its musk of seasoned oak. Of the lime on the damp walls.

They regarded each other over breakfast. Coy at their beginning. Startled by its freshness and colour. Too stiff a cloth to be comfortable yet.

Argus picked up the vibrations. Ever alert, ever sensitive, he watched them from his sick bed with those lambent, intelligent eyes. The run up to the quarry the day before had done him no good. It was too soon for such adventure. But he wore his hurt with grace. Pride even, in his exploits, seeing as his master had emerged unscathed.

They spent the day at the cottage. Pottering here and there. She showed him all over her land. The little bog where the snipe nested. The stand of ghostly, ancient beech. The green lane beneath the oak trees leading up over the hill, away from the mystery of the valley towards the hard upland light. They rolled up their trousers to splash in the stream. There was a mini-waterfall, and beneath it the dish of a smooth rockpool where they stood and grinned at one another. Feelings bubbled to the surface, now that they could.

Argus came too. He made a few scentings, but his heart wasn't in them. Mostly he watched the man and how he was with the girl. Not resentful but rather sensitive of change and seeking understanding.

The man felt his love ferment. Even as the adrenalin of his voyage drained itself into the deep peace of his surroundings, at the same time a new excitement built inside him for the future. Love, friendship, homeliness. These were new wonders.

He attacked the weeds growing near the cottage, wielding an ancient scythe and trying not to slice off his own leg. He took his revenge on the entire world of the stinging nettle. Just being amongst them revived the rash he carried around his neck from the night at the quarry. The girl found him before he had them all cut down at his feet. She said leave some for the butterflies, and the other insects.

They had lunch sitting on the bench in front of the cottage. A little table spread with bread, cheese and some salad from her garden. A bowl of yoghurt mixed with heather honey from the Moor.

The surroundings were powerful for both. She loved their familiarity, and the memory they held of her labour. She loved the three great oaks on the steep slope opposite, standing impassive and unshakable. They made her feel small in a happy way. They made sense somehow of frantic human striving and all things perishable. Whereas for him, the newness and the originality sparkled, as it couldn't for her. He breathed in each new impression, eager to exhaust the first ones and exchange them for a second and a third breath. After the wildness of the quarry, he felt himself drawn in by the cosy convenience of it all, slightly against his will. Such feelings seemed disloyal to his recent home.

In the afternoon, he wheeled the lawnmower from its cobwebbed corner of the barn and set about taming her lawn. The request was unspoken. He sensed that she would be pleased not to have to do it, even though she easily could. He felt himself watched from the kitchen window as he tramped up and down in shorts and bare feet, dancing round the thistles. It must be strange for her, he thought, to look out on a man at work in her domain. He guessed at her mix reaction. He should be careful not to presume.

In truth, she was too at ease with herself and her valley to feel threatened or invaded by his work. By his need to work, to establish his place in that tiny world. Rather, she found it endearing how he sought to enter the simple hierarchy through payment of goodwill.

Later, they walked over to a ridge on the western skyline, with its knarled avenue of Scots Pine. From there, they looked back towards the cottage, sheltered by the two great folds of land to north and south. The change of scale was surprising. Down there, they felt as if they saw as much of the earth as ever they would need to see. Up on the ridge, they could only just pick out the cottage, hidden in its combe, as their eyes scanned the horizon.

31.

He cycled off to work at the campsite the next morning. Argus would not be left behind. The girl waved them off.

It was delicious. Belonging. Leaving with the certain prospect of returning soon. A figure framed in a doorway with a ready greeting. An inkling of home. But he was not deceived. He knew how returns diminished. The brightest beginning might one day make for the dullest routine. Besides, Judy was a ghostly impression hidden behind every thought. He would never settle until he found her.

At the campsite, Argus kept close. The hound sensed the displacement looming. Approaching the holidays, there were more campers and plenty of tidying to do after them. The grass grew with such determination. The great oak over the main building was fully in leaf, gathering all under its wings. Argus lay on the dry, rooted ground beneath it and watched the mower's dressage around him. As the man manoeuvred about, nodding gently on his sprung seat above the roller, he prepared the avowal he would make in the office after work.

When the moment came, he searched about for any excuse but found none. Once he stood before the old man's soft benevolence he knew his anxiety was out of place. There was nothing to be found on earth which this ancient being did not embrace with compassion and understanding.

'You've seen the mess I made up at the quarry. I'm sorry about that. It's all filled in again now. I suppose I should speak to the Sisters about it. Try and explain. Or maybe you have already.'

The old man smoothed away his guilt.

'They know what they need to know. But it wouldn't hurt for you to say hello one day.'

'I'm staying over at the farm now. In case I'd worn out my welcome with them. I need to be off travelling sometime soon, and I've been worrying about how to tell you. It feels like I'm letting you down, what with the high season not far off. But I must go and find my daughter. I haven't seen her, or heard from her, in over seven years. Now that I can, I want to find her.'

The old man regarded him. Connected and loving.

'Go when you like, with my blessing. Bring her here one day to meet us. And have no fear for the campsite. There's a young lad in the village, just doing his exams. I've had my eye on him for a while now. He'll do very well for the summer holidays. He's capable and conscientious.'

They looked at each other quietly. Neither spoke. The thoughts passed unsaid. The old man's gaze fell upon Argus and his wound.

'What'll you do with the hound?'

The question revived the guilt. He had no ready answer. Could he, should he take him? As for the girl, nothing more had been discussed. Another departure, and the complications were mounting. No wonder people preferred to stay put.

He took a roundabout route back to the farm with Argus alongside. Up over the hill past the quarry entrance. They stopped there on the road but didn't go in. The man sat astride his bicycle, propped on one leg, and looked along the path. Already the brambles and stinging nettles and sapling leaves had covered his tracks and woven together a barrier of exclusion. The movement of the earth was so relentless. He felt no longer welcome.

Argus was quizzical. Nothing to do but wait for a new scent. A new direction. Eventually he cast about for himself and set off down the hill towards the Georgian house. The man was grateful for the lead.

In the field beside the road, where once he had seen the Sisters bent in toil, there they were again. This time in the company of a cohort of friends. The group ranged in age from the very young to the venerable, all stooped over ridges of soil to plant late potatoes. The Sisters' winter staple. He recognised some of the faces from the village.

They were too intent upon their task to notice him peering over the hedge. So much the better, for he found himself suddenly moved by this vision set against the blue and white of an early summer sky. People together, working in the fields, united and cooperative. He was so used to the drone of machinery on the land. To hear voices and laughter instead came upon him like the beauty of a dawn chorus.

They belonged in that field in a way that he doubted he ever would. Ever could. No matter. He might dance with delusion this once. He pushed his bicycle along to a gateway and left it there against the hedge. In the field, Argus set off straightaway to make new acquaintance, beginning with the very young. His hispid good nature was irresistible, and he knew it. The man made his way over to where the sisters were at work, amongst the venerable. He made no effort towards explanation or introduction. He just smiled and offered his help. They were unquestioning. They gave him a hoe and a bag of seed potatoes and he joined himself to their tableau.
The work of conscience was unremitting, or so it seemed. The revolution of his world remorseless. Yet for an hour all that ceased. He moved to one side, and for a brief interlude he was the puppeteer,

85

not the puppet. He felt integrated in a way he had never known before. Argus as always his passport to ease and acceptance. The man joined their banter, sensed the strength of their spirit and their muddy purpose. Their contentment.

When the job was done, the workers gathered into an excited, noisy bunch and moved off towards the house. One of the Sisters approached him, with an invitation to join them for tea. He said no thankyou, he was expected. She reached up her hand to touch his face.

32.

'How long is it since you had that lorry going?'
She stared through him as she tried to remember.
'When I first moved into the house, I used to start it regularly, say once a month, and leave the engine running for a while. Somebody told me that's what you're supposed to do. I still thought I might need it. But the MOT ran out, then the insurance was too expensive to renew. I suppose it must be over a year since I last started it up.'
'Everything was in working order, though, when you last tried?'
'Yes. It used to fire up, no problem. Except the battery had to be charged, sometimes.'
'I'd like to fetch some petrol, and try to get the engine running. See what sort of condition it's in. Is that OK?'
'Yes. Of course.'
She thought at first that he was just trying to be useful. Pay his way. Do the things he knew how to do. Later, when he had gone out on the bicycle with the empty petrol can strapped to his rear carrier, she wondered whether there mightn't be an ulterior motive.

He returned with fuel and some tools borrowed from the campsite. He connected the battery to a charger. The needle showed a steady current, which was a good sign. He checked the fan belt, oil and water levels, clutch and brakes. The brake pedal felt spongy, but that wasn't surprising. When he was satisfied it could do no harm, he reconnected the battery and put half the petrol he had bought into the tank.

He sat in the driver's seat and felt quite excited. Ignition on and the petrol pump clicked into life. After a few seconds he turned the key and listened closely to the engine turning over. It wasn't seized, at least, but it didn't fire either. He switched off to save the battery. Next, he cleaned up the points and the spark plugs, pouring a little neat petrol into each cylinder. There was a good spark, she had to go now. He called the girl and got her to turn the key this time, in case it made a difference.

The lorry coughed, spluttered and backfired into combustion. They cheered and hugged each other with childish grins, though they didn't quite know why. He poured in the rest of the petrol and revved until the engine was thoroughly warm and running as it should.

So far so encouraging. He reversed out of the barn into the yard. He needed daylight to make a close inspection underneath the chassis. The tyres were down, but not badly worn or perished. The cover of the barn had kept the worst of the rust at bay. Only the brake pipes and cylinders would need attention. And maybe the shoes.

He found her sitting at the table.
'I know you've guessed by now. I want us to take the lorry. Begin looking on the continent where it's likeliest they'll be. I can do the work on the brakes myself, and get her through the MOT. I could pay the insurance monthly, so there's only a small amount to find. The tax is free. The worst would be the ferry, and the petrol, but I have a little saved for that. We could take Argus in the back. Hide him if necessary. And there's room for our bikes. It's perfect for what we need.'
She smiled her indulgence. He guessed why.
'OK. It's perfect for what I need. But you would enjoy it too. When did you last get away from here? Not that you need to

get away, I know. At least, when you return you can see it with fresh eyes, like you crave to do. Your enthusiasm will be renewed, your sense of the place all the stronger after you have tramped about in Europe for a while.'

She remained thoughtful. Unconvinced. He left silence, sensing that it would count against him if he pressed harder. Eventually she stood up.

'Please go ahead and do the work. See if you can get an MOT. It's only right that you should. I've felt awkward for a while now, seeing the lorry abandoned and unused in the barn. You have a good use in mind, and I'm pleased to see it cared for again, by someone who knows how. You must take it. It's yours. But I haven't decided yet what I shall do.'

He knew her better than to argue. She understood herself too well to be pressurised. He decided to get busy with the mechanics, and leave other matters to resolve themselves. What pleasure there was sometimes in the sharp physical world of things. A happy refuge from the steam of thought, with its endless condensation in the brain.

He jacked up the chassis, removed the wheels and let the weight settle on wooden blocks. The sections of brake pipe that showed signs of corrosion he removed so as to get them copied. One brake cylinder would have to be repaired. The shoes and drums he needed only to clean up and they might pass inspection.

He was happy in his work. Excited at where it was leading. He allowed himself to imagine the future. A reunion. The idea made his hands tremble. He had to put down the tools and walk away. In search of composure.

33.

The coming journey was divisive. They could not recapture the closeness of their first embrace.

The man threw all his energy into renovating the lorry. When he had reconditioned the brakes, he booked an appointment for an MOT and arranged insurance on the telephone. He turned his attention to the interior. There was already a wooden sleeping platform at the back, beneath a little sliding window which was cut into the rear panel. He enlarged and modified this area, so that there was a concealed compartment underneath the bed in which he could hide Argus if necessary. He drilled through the floor to ensure it was well ventilated.

The lorry had three roof windows, which let in plenty of light and could be opened to prevent the inside getting too stuffy. There was a folding side door with steps up, through which the public had come, once upon a time, to select books from their mobile library. He converted the issue counter behind the driver's seat into a little kitchenette, with a double gas burner and a small round sink salvaged from the recycling centre. The wooden shelving, which had housed the books, would be useful for general storage and display.

He needed to be busy to control his excitement. Once he had allowed the thoughts of Judy to play in his head, he could no longer contain or control them.

The girl understood this, but it did not help her. She had no means of sharing this part of him. There was no way in. His energy and enthusiasm for the trip ahead endeared him to her but she could not artificially recreate them for herself. However hard she tried to remain open, she could not but feel a little excluded.

This man had sacrificed seven years of his life to protect his family. How churlish it would be to begrudge him freedom now. Yet this man had also penetrated into her quiet isolation, and she feared its equilibrium had been taken from her. If she let him leave now without her, how would it be afterwards? Might not solitude turn to loneliness?

She had constructed a world of self-sufficiency, both practical and emotional. There were compromises hidden in such a retreat. But when she relaxed her guard and welcomed this man in she took a risk. Now she sensed the full danger of that welcome. The inhabitants of an isolated area have poor resistance to infection from outside.

In the end she would agree to go with him. This much she knew. A picture had come to mind, of herself in a boat on the lake, alone and palely loitering. No, such a role would not amuse or nourish her. The antipathy she felt towards the tragic heroines was profound.

For now, she said nothing of this to the man. There was pleasure in watching him at work, so careful and thorough. He didn't attack machinery, as she had seen so many men do, as if it was a challenge to their masculinity. Rather he seemed to massage its parts back to useful life. She observed him slyly from behind a window or a tree, his forearms and shirt filmed with dust or black with grease. It was as sensual a vision as any she had known. Partly for the way it suggested an intrusion into her sanctuary. Partly for the honesty and purpose at work.

The lorry failed its inspection on account of a loose wheel bearing and a worn steering joint. The man was undaunted. He ordered the bearing and searched through scrap yards until he could replace the joint. The second time he drove back up the lane beaming with pride and waving the certificate out of the window. Argus had taken to sitting on the passenger seat. His manner had at first been a little self-conscious and uncertain, but now he looked out imperiously as once he had done from the wheelbarrow. He carried his confidence with such easy instinct, and the result was all conquering. It was what made him a good companion.

The sight of the old lorry grinding its cautious way about the lanes became a familiar one to other local traffic. The man felt the need for thorough trialling before he set off across the Channel. He grew accustomed to the looks of surprise, bafflement and sometimes terror on the faces of oncoming motorists as they registered the majesty of Argus staring down at them through the tall lorry windscreen.

He went to the library in order to look up ferry timetables and prices on the internet. He found a cheap one-way crossing at an unsocial hour. It was the only one he could afford, before the price hike of the summer holidays.

34.

They began their journey early one morning in midweek. The man had said his goodbyes at the campsite. His final pay packet contained a bonus for 'petrol money', so the old man explained it.

The girl had arranged at the last minute for the farmer to look after the cottage. He would be there anyway to check on his animals. The lawn and the garden might grow a little wild, but no matter. She emptied the greenhouse of all that she could take, and dug up a stock of vegetables which she placed in a wicker basket. With that, a large bag of rice and a sack of dog biscuit, they might live in the lorry very cheaply. She sorted out some old pots and pans and plates of no value. He made a store of essential tools and spare parts.

Argus had to yield his front seat to the girl, which he did with good grace. He took to lying instead on the bed platform at the back, from where he could look out through the small square opening at the unfortunate motorists stuck behind them. If anything, this arrangement was more dangerous than the first. His jovial face framed by the window was a powerful distraction. Queues built up and the overtaking became erratic. There were toots and waves as cars came past. It seemed Argus had the power to disarm even road rage. The man allowed himself a smile, but otherwise made no acknowledgement. He was locked steadfast onto the task ahead.

It took a while for the girl to settle into the moment, after the swirl of departure. The magic of setting out on a voyage absorbed her apprehensions. Her unease was replaced by sharp excitement. The motion of the wheels and the leisure of being driven removed responsibility. A decision had been made. Now she would enjoy her role.

They headed through chalk country towards the coast. For lunch they turned off into the lanes and found a spot high on a ridge where they could park up for a while. There were views all around of unchallenged gold and yellow. Argus took them exploring up an ancient drover's track.

By evening, they came close to the ferry port. They stopped in countryside above the city. Their sailing was not until after midnight.

'I think I'll take the bike out and give Argus another run while it's still light. He'll want to stretch his legs if he's spending the night cooped up under the bed. Are you coming?'

The girl hesitated. Was it a genuine invitation, or a polite formality?

'No. You go. Is it necessary, all this subterfuge? Surely you must be able to travel with a dog on the way out, even if there are restrictions coming back.'

He frowned.

'Why take the risk? They might not let us on the boat, if he has no papers, and no microchip. I don't want to have to come back again. It'll do no harm to hide him.'

Whilst they were gone the girl made her first attempt at cooking a hot meal using the new kitchenette. Space was limited, but she admired the man's ingenuity. Compact and purposeful in everything. She felt her uneasiness returning, now that the wheels were idle. For as long as they spun, she was a passenger on the move, seduced by ever-changing scenery. Her thoughts and impressions clamoured for attention, fresh and varied. Her mind was so busy processing, it let

go the usual obsessions. Best of all was the comfort of passi·
Somebody else had a plan, a purpose. For as long as they drove, tᵤₑᵣₑ
was no getting off. The interminable chorus of futility was silent.

But when the wheels stopped, the tedious noises all began again. Just
like the moment she pushed through the swing doors of an auditorium
after the performance to find the old grey reality awaiting her outside.
However long the music played or the images flickered, her brain's
monstrous eye was occupied elsewhere, swivelled outwards. When
the doors swung to behind her and she moved out into the street,
she sensed the eye rotate to resume its chill inward scrutiny. She
wasn't alone in that, she felt sure. Although many of those in the
audience seemed impatient to be up and away at the end, back to the
reassurance of their routines, there were always others like her who
lingered. Who clung to the last frame or note before the crush of
responsibility filled the void. If the performance was good enough, it
could send her on her way with an enveloping force field to keep the
humdrum burdens at bay. Sometimes for hours, sometimes for days.

Alone, in a stationary lorry, she knew all too well what made her
uneasy. She was warm and clean and comfortable. Her independence
sufficiently flattered by the mode of travel. She loved. But she wasn't
sure of being loved.

Of her requirements for living, this one she had charmed to sleep. The
compromise of the solitary. Now the man had trampled over her spell.
The need to be loved was aggrieved and demanding. Nothing but the
most intense attention would do, to make up for the past denial.

During the early, heady days the man had more than satisfied. Now
she felt his attention wander. He thought of finding his daughter. He
hardened to his task. It wasn't that his feelings had diminished, she
told herself. Rather that the heat of his love began to dissipate with
the journey. How unreasonable it would be to object to that, after a
seven year separation from his child. Yet she did object. She was
jealous of Judy.

35.

The sea was mid-summer calm. The crossing went without incident. When first they drove onto the car deck, they made a show of gathering their possessions to move to the upper levels along with the other drivers. But when the crew were occupied elsewhere, they hid inside the lorry and kept quiet until everyone had gone. The man was afraid Argus might howl if left alone, and since they couldn't afford a cabin it was the best chance they had of a good night's rest.

In the morning, they stayed out of sight until drivers were requested to return to their vehicles. Then there wasn't time to leave the lorry, so they never got to see the ferry or the sea.

The effect was unsettling. In normal circumstances they would have watched the lights of their homeland fade into the distance. They would have smelt the salt air and quaked at the endless grey of the waves. Patrolling the rusty gangways their minds would have had time to adjust.

As it was, they breathed only oil and bilge fumes. They emerged from the ship's womb confused and disorientated. The man remembered to sidle to the right, as he tugged at the steering wheel with hands dampened by fear. They drove an unusual vehicle, so Customs might decide to check on them. When they reached the control point, it was deserted. They could just accelerate off into the early morning mist.

The streets of the town were quiet still. Only the bars and newsagents showed any sign of business. The faces of the buildings were so very different somehow. It took a while to understand why. Their stare was blind, every eye lidded with wood, steel or PVC. Only when they awoke would the houses and flats blink to let in the daylight. Even then, some of them would remain shuttered forever against the heat of a midday sun.

It was their first impression of the continental approach. Earnest, and above all practical. They felt foreign and exposed in their slow, impractical lorry. They headed straight for the countryside, where a blanket of green and gold might cover their nakedness. And where Argus, who was bursting, might be let out for a run.

All three of them were glad to break away into the freshness of a country morning. The sun had burnt off the mists by the time they cycled for the first time on that land mass stretching infinitely East and South. The strangeness and the scale were intimidating. It was tempting to scream and rush back home again. Even Argus hesitated for an instant, as his nose pulled in the vast new world around him. But only a moment's pause, with one leg pointing the way South, before he plunged on down the lane.

They hurried after to catch up and re-educate his notion of left and right. Since he was usually to be found on the wrong side at home they had hopes that he might be more on the right side over here. But his nonchalance on the highway defied any such logic. He was too busy running at life to worry about the line of his attack.

Everything they saw that morning remained with them long after, radiating the halogen memory of excitement and discovery. The monstrous cattle knee deep in grass, the poultry foraging by the roadside, the farmsteads spewing out into the hamlets instead of hidden down private tracks. The peasant greeting seemed straight forward and yet somehow epic.

They stopped at a bakery to buy a large round loaf weighing more than a kilo. Its chewy sourdough texture was still fresh days later. The man had to cling to Argus to keep him from raiding the display of cakes. Meanwhile the hound was much admired by grizzled hunting men who dreamed away the summer until the chase might begin again.

They returned to the lorry. In the quiet of their chosen lay-by, they sprawled in the sunshine eating bread and honey with slices of cool fruit. The confusion of their arrival had given way to a goofy contentment. Would that every day began just like this one. The man forgot his search and the girl felt her anxiety evaporate into the surrounding heat.

Desire could spin them apart, but now it spun them together. The langourous air inside the lorry made them cast aside their clothes in a way that might have been awkward at home. Here, they felt urged on, applauded even by their surroundings. Passion was tinged not with guilt but with despair. They would never find a way to sustain such happiness.

36.

For three days they headed South, following the same pattern. The man was reluctant to motor in the middle of the day, in case the engine overheated. So they travelled during the cool of morning and evening, for about four hours at a time. They looked forward to the break in the middle of the day, when they could find a quiet spot to park up, deep in the countryside.

Each time, they sampled a different region by bicycle, as if theirs was a tasting tour. From inside the lorry, the view of the passing landscape was as good as it could be. But it wasn't fulfilling. The noise of the engine and the barrier of metal and glass was always an underlying frustration. By mid morning they were impatient to be out on two wheels. Only then could they be at one with the land they voyaged through. Only then could they satisfy the appetite of their senses. To smell the air, laden with harvest or livestock, to hear snatches of birdsong or dialect, to experience close-to the daily routines of parish life. This was their way to fuse with the surroundings, and the bicycle served as catalyst in that fusion.

After a few hours pedalling and appeasement, they would return to the lorry, famished and bearing some item of local produce which they bought each day as a treat. The pleasure was not just in the eating, it was in the purchase too. To knock at a farm door, or stop at a village stores became a childish delight. Their encounters made them giggling conspirators, forever redeemed by the bonhomie of Argus.

By early evening, fed and rested, they were pleased to move on again and try to outrun the dying rhythm of the day. The first time he drove on into the twilight, the man was convinced something was wrong with the lorry. He could hear a loud chirr, which he imagined to be a faulty bearing or a worn belt. He tried to ignore it, willing the problem to resolve itself. When eventually he stopped to investigate, he found the trouble was in his own foolishness. The sound he heard was that of a thousand cicadas, revelling in the warmth of a summer night.

In three days they covered a distance which they might have achieved in a single day on the motorway. But they preferred their loose stitch to the rent of high speed travel.

The honeymoon was loving, but brief. As they approached the South, their mission reasserted itself. The man grew nervous. What had seemed so easy from afar now looked ridiculous.

'I've based this whole venture on wishful thinking. I don't suppose I need to tell you that, but I see it now, for myself.'

'I didn't want to take away your hope. Yet I wonder what it is you think you'll find. These friends of Judy's mother, you said you visited them once with her. What do you know of them?'

'Of her friends, very little. But the village where they lived, that I do remember. It had an amazing view of a mountain. You looked down to the end of this steep-sided valley, across the flood plain of a river and there standing over you was this huge mass of granite, with twin peaks 3000 metres high. And the houses were all falling down. The place was ghostly. You'll see.'

'Is that where we're headed?'

'I thought we might camp nearby. There's a forest higher up in the valley behind the village. From there we can explore by bike.' They were silent again. The sun had set over the foothills of a great mountain range. It was not far now, and the man decided to push on into the dark so that he could wake up where for so long he had dreamt of waking. To look out of the window the next morning and have a view of that mountain, which haunted him still. That was everything he longed for just then. Everything he allowed himself to long for.

It was a bad plan. He followed road signs to the town, but after that he had to try and find his way by memory, in the dark. He got lost in the narrow lanes, and began to question his own judgement more and more. The girl felt him drowning, but couldn't save him. He stopped at a house to ask the way. They were suspicious of a stranger late at night, especially one with a foreign accent asking the way to a forest. They shook their heads and frowned.

The man was desperate, but still determined. It was the first time that the girl gained a true appreciation of the reserves he held somewhere out of sight. He didn't rant, or despair, or lose his temper. He set off again quickly, on his search, and the girl felt a lifejacket of purpose and self-belief inflate itself around him.

It was very late when the man found the road he was looking for. It ran past several farms along the ridge of a hill into a dead end. A rough stone track continued as far as a clearing at the edge of the forest. There they parked. From the ridge you could see down over the tops of the trees as far as the sacred mountain. The man was satisfied at last. His smile was self-mocking. The girl had not liked to speak for fear of provoking him. But that smile told her so much which she didn't know. His balance, his self-awareness, they were as sound as hers. She might do as she pleased, since it wouldn't unsettle him.

She knew now why she had come. To be thrown together with another person, under pressure on an adventure. That was the best way to intimate knowledge and understanding. To squeeze at very beginning until you could taste the other's essence, and so avoiu years of sullen disillusion later.

37.

When he woke around dawn, the man rolled over onto his front. He was rewarded with a rare vision. If he had driven all night in search of this, it would still have been worth it.

The sun rose somewhere behind him, colouring the mountain deep red before it struck the surrounding country. He could make out the fiery twin peaks, and the ancient castle stronghold atop a pog of rock at the base. The low country was black and white, only the mountain was stained blood red. The whole was double-framed, by the sharp undulation of the valley's end, and by the square of the lorry's rear window.

The girl was sleeping, her breath quiet and even. He kissed her. Her eyelids opened long enough to see him point towards the window. Long enough to register the dawn view, before they closed again to seal in her sleep.
He went out with Argus, and wandered along the forest tracks, beneath a canopy of evergreen oak and pine. He remembered walking there eleven years before, when Judy had showed clearly as a mound bursting through her mother's summer dress. They had gone for a stroll as a foursome, after a chatty lunch on the terrace. He tried to picture their hosts, but the faces were empty of detail. The husband a struggling writer. The wife rather loud and bossy. If they still lived in the village, the chances were that they didn't know anything. And no reason to tell a convicted murderer, even if they did.

It was the preparation for this trip that had offered the most. The optimism and the euphoria, the unreasoned hope, the excitement of coming adventure, he could feel them all slink away to await another beginning. Henceforth, he would have to rely upon determination. And love.

By late morning they were ready to set off bicycling on their search. They coasted downhill along forest tracks towards the village, inspired by the vigour of swift movement and the attendance of the trees. There was discovery to be had from the day.

At the centre of the houses was a great level wasteland, surrounded by a tumbling wall. Here the last of the doomed family of Counts had lived, until mounting dilapidations led to the destruction of his ancient chateau. He spent the remainder of his days exiled from his home and evading his debtors, until at the age of sixty he surrendered to life and poisoned himself.

They leant their bicycles against the Church wall, and wandered through the village, tasting the sadness and the despair. Some of the houses had been renovated, but many were still empty and abandoned. They exchanged pleasantries with an old lady who was tending her garden. She showed an interest in the visitors, and told them how the Count haunted the area still, galloping his horses at night down the main street in an attempt to outpace the dull republican forces.

The man had made no plan. Suddenly they were walking past a house he recognised from its front terrace. He stopped and felt his heart accelerate beyond control. He had stumbled into a moment which could decide the future.

Argus pushed through a half-open front gate into the garden. Reaction, as so often, took the place of action. The man lunged forwards to capture the hound and then retreat. But a woman stepped out of open french windows to greet them. When the man looked up from struggling to get a hand hold on Argus their eyes met. The woman's polite humour addled into ugly recognition. She spoke to release her fear.

       'I thought you were ...'

The man cut in. He did not want to hear it.

'I was. But I'm out now. Have been for several months. Where are they?'

He had not meant to be so blunt. The chit-chat wouldn't come. The woman made as if to answer, then turned and stepped back into the house. He was left holding onto Argus and feeling very alone. He looked towards the girl, but she had walked on out of view.

He would wait for his answer. He had forever. There were voices from inside the house. He invited himself to sit down at the garden table. Show resolution. Take time to regain some composure. Presently the woman emerged. She was followed by a youthful-looking husband, who made as if to stretch out a hand in greeting, but stopped himself and then opened his mouth to conceal an awkwardness.

The man stayed seated at the table. He held up a hand. The gesture was expressive. It sued for peace. It pleaded to be heard.

'I don't know what you've been told. It really doesn't matter to me any more. But before you speak, please believe this. I have never done deliberate harm to anyone, and I mean to continue that way. All I want is to see my daughter.'

The husband looked perplexed, compassionate even but he remained silent. His wife would speak for them both, as she was accustomed to do.

'They're not here. We haven't heard from them in ages. We don't know where they are.'

The man considered this for a while.

'Which suggests to me that they were here, once?'

The woman was caught in headlights. She sniffed.

'Yes. They came here after the trial. They stayed with us. Both of them needed a little quiet and security. But they moved on, of their own accord.'

The man sensed that there was more. He leaned back in the chair to show that he would wait. The woman turned to go back in.

'Try the market on Monday. There's a stallholder there who sells her own cheese. She may tell you more.'

38.

They cycled into town early on market day. The traders were busy pulling tables, awnings and boxes of goods from the back of grubby vans. The wealthier types had specially converted lorries, which opened up to form refrigerated counters of meat or fish or cheese. On another, the sides were covered in rotating spits, which skewered a hundred roasting chickens. From broiler to free range to organic, pay your money and take your pick.

There were fruit and vegetables and flowers from the surrounding country. Bread and pastries from half a dozen individual bakers. Cheap clothes. A lorry full of hats. Pottery, woodwork and in one corner, where the farmers gossiped, all manner of live poultry and caged rabbits.

The man held hands with the girl. They wandered in the early morning sunshine and marvelled at such a land of plenty. It might have been like any other cornucopia, except that this one was thronged each week by eccentrics of every hue. And the whole was held together within the boundaries of a market square which had not changed in five hundred years. On three sides were half-timbered medieval houses, with a broad continuous cloister propped on pillars of rough oak. It concealed a line of shops set well back in the shade. The fourth side of the square was formed by the north wall of an elegant Gothic Cathedral. It turned its back on mammon, yet all the while suggested a path for the repentant through its massive studded doors.

Some of the smaller traders gathered under the roof of a central pavilion, each standing behind a little table of eggs or wool or flowers with an air of self-conscious disdain. The man lingered in this area, on the lookout for a woman selling cheese. The girl had gone to sit at a café and try to restrain Argus, who threatened to cause havoc amongst the stalls with his excess of nose, tail and goodwill to all.

The man joined them after a while. He seemed tense.

'I don't think I can do this. There's too much at stake. Will you go?'

'Have you seen her?'

'There's someone over in the far corner, selling little round goat's cheeses from a glass cabinet. But I haven't talked to her. I know I'll say the wrong thing, or get aggressive and mess it up. Please, you go. This needs a woman's touch. You speak the language better.'

She thought about refusing such a slithery appeal. But his smile was too faltering and boyish. It left no room for no. She might take on his responsibility this once.

Her approach was cautious. She watched the trading from a distance, and tried to gain an understanding of the woman's life. There were friendly conversations with purchasers, as if her clients were regulars. It all seemed quite happy and relaxed. Smiles on each side, pleasantries with neighbouring stallholders, a steady flow of trade. The girl became confident that straightforward honesty would work best.

'How much are those soft cheeses?'

'Three euros each. Or you can have two for five euros, if you like.'

The woman was sharp. She had noticed a new face. It was worth a discount to hook another regular. This girl fitted her typical customer profile.

'I'm only passing through. But I'll take the two, please.'

The woman wrapped the cheeses in stiff waxed paper to protect them. The girl caught her eye as she handed over a bank note. There was a twinkle of respect on both sides. A commercial manoeuvre had been acknowledged.

'I've been watching you for a bit. You seem to do alright here. I do prefer goat's cheese, because it's easier to digest, especially when you're on the move. But that's not why I'm buying. I expect you've guessed from my accent where I come from. I'm here with a friend. He's looking for his daughter, Judy.'

She had found the right place. No doubt of that. The woman reacted with instinctive recoil. Not unfriendly, but guarded certainly, possibly even defensive.

'I knew her. Her mother helped with the goats. They lived in a gite on my farm for over a year. But there was some trouble when they left. I do not hear from them now.'

It was said in conclusion, bordering on dismissal.

'You're busy. I must leave you to get on with your market.'

The girl picked up a leaflet from a pile on the table. It gave information on the cheese production, and the farm where the goats were kept.

'Perhaps we could come and visit you, if that's OK.'

She waved the leaflet.

'If you like.'

It was not an encouragement. The woman turned to another customer.

When she rejoined the man, they left the square and headed down side streets away from the throng. The centre of the town was laid out in a grid of well-fashioned ancient houses. The muddle and confusion of the century had made no impact on this confident order. Whereas outside the ring road all was a chaos of cement. They admired the detail of a stone mullion or a vaulted arch. The doorways were broad and elaborate. The man's attention was caught by some letters on one lintel, dated four hundred years back in time. VERITAS ODIUM PARIT. He stopped to consider. What was it in the life of this householder that had inspired him to carve such an inscription.?

'How's your Latin?'

The girl crossed the street to look more closely.

' Something about the truth hurts, truthful people tending to make enemies.'

'I wonder what happened here in this town in someone's life. It's not about religious truth. Imagine a person who spoke his mind, and made himself unpopular. He was alienated, an outsider say, yet he continued to live in the centre of town. And was sufficiently prosperous to have this carved on his doorway, as a way of sticking up two fingers to his neighbours. A medieval raspberry.'

'A bit depressing, though, don't you think? That such things don't change. Enlightenment is followed by years of treading in stale, brutish circles. And truth chases feelgood away.'

The man reached out to bunch the girl's hair in his hands, then feed it through his fingers.

'Right now, I'm not depressed. Increasingly desperate, maybe. But how could I feel depressed whilst I'm still in mid-adventure?'

39.

They set off early by bicycle, across the river's flood plain into the dense woodland of the foothills. The man had bought a map of the area, so that they might avoid the main roads and follow instead the lanes in quiet safety.

They were headed straight towards the mountain. Coming round a corner or reaching a little summit, they would be presented with a view southwards so startling or full of awe that it was hard to fill lungs flattened by exertion. For those who lived with it, it was always there. But for them, the energy and excitement were boundless and new. Including Argus, who kept stopping to twitch at the air as if he didn't quite believe what it was he sensed there. He rushed forwards, covering the ground with an effortless lope. Had they not kept going with him, they felt he would have carried on regardless.

The scale was ever changing. The closer they came to the mountain, the less they could see of it, but the more they sensed its presence. The foothills at the base were increasingly steep. Their uphill progress slowed to a walking pace. The view was now of the valleys running off the bottom, steep-sided and filled with the torrents of melted snow. One great rock rose above the rest, a thumb of granite holding aloft a fortress of castellated stone. An impregnable stronghold, except through starvation. One generation of its inhabitants had surrendered after years of siege. Their religious crime was to declare this life irredeemable, and to await salvation in the next. They trudged down to the base of the rock in their hundreds, tired and emaciated but not defeated. They were offered freedom if they renounced their creed. They chose instead the auto-da-fe, and were burnt together on a huge funeral pyre. The persecutors can't have noticed that by torturing their victims to death they confirmed the rightfulness of the martyrs' beliefs.

Such passion haunted the surroundings still. It found its way into the hearts of the man and the girl. It fired their legs as they cranked a way higher, towards the remote upland farm where the woman milked goats to make her cheese. They followed a no-through road, as it zigzagged its route past pine forest to reach a clearing on the mountain's flank.

At the top they were rewarded. The view was no longer up, it was down and across. Down into the valley beneath, where the last of the morning mist was claimed by the sun, and where they could see the comings and goings of the village in miniature. Across the plain, northwards for miles and miles, the way they had come. Most wonderful of all was the sight of the rock fortress. Dislocated from the earth by the last of the mists, it floated on the air as a heavenly memorial to the martyrdom it had inspired.

It was a special place. Energy tingled through every feature. The man understood why Judy and her mother might have lived here. For the first time he felt he was really on their trail. He wanted to cry out his discovery, as Argus might have done amidst the pack.
The farmhouse was set into the mountain rock, facing south. To one side was the old stone barn, which had been converted into a gite. A new timber shed had been built down in the corner of the meadow, where the goats were housed. There was a dairy to one side.

They stood taking it all in, in no hurry to make contact. The power there seemed to force linear time to one side.
    'I can see her now. I can hear her giggles and feel her tears when she falls over. It's silly, I know, but this is as close as I have been for so long. I want to stay here and relive the moments with her that I have missed.'
He was overwhelmed suddenly by the thought of his loss. Her young

childhood would never be his memory. Tears of anguish came to his eyes, leaking away the compressed sadness of their separation.

They heard a door closing down at the goatshed. A figure made its way up the path towards the farmhouse. They recognised the woman from the market. She stopped for a moment when she saw them, then continued her climb.

Her look softened when she noticed the man's distress. She made a fuss of Argus, and still no-one spoke. There was no room for polite formalities. She was sympathetic. She made an effort to synchronise her mood with theirs.

'It was lovely to have Judy here. I miss her childish fun. Of course, I have my goats for company, but it's not the same. Let me offer you something to drink. You must be thirsty after such a cycle.'

They sat on a little terrace in front of the house, in the dappled shade of a vine. The land fell away sharply to the west, giving a view of valley and village, woodland and mountain so varied and beautiful that the eye could not rest in its contemplation. There was too much to see. The light on the contours was forever changing.

'How can you live everyday in this place? The wonder of it is just too agonising.'

The man stared and stared out from the terrace, and still he was incredulous.

'When I first came here, I couldn't believe it was for real. That I should live and work in such a spot. But now on certain days I catch myself taking it for granted. I have to leave and then come back again, in order to recharge the spell. It gets more difficult, the more my brain discounts the magic.'

Her words gave way to a wry smile. The woman knew that once she had offered hospitality, she was bound to give this man some account of his daughter and her mother. She did not wish to relive the unhappiness, yet she could not turn away from his entreaty.

'We met first at the market, and got on well together. She said she was looking for somewhere to live with Judy, but couldn't afford much rent. I spoke of the gite, which is usually empty after the summer holidays. I thought it might be good to have some company over the winter. Judy was so adorable, and I have no children of my own. Except for my goats. Her mother agreed to work on the farm to pay the rent.

'To begin with, it went well. We took Judy down to the school in the village. She had such enthusiasm for her learning. We lived almost like a family. But then her mother began an affair with a local man. He is well-known around here. He is not a good person. She did less and less to help me, but still she paid no rent. She changed. She became someone I was not happy to know.

'For Judy's sake I could not ask them to leave. The child had so little security, yet she seemed always cheerful and loving. It is for her sake that I talk of what I do not wish to remember.

'They left one time when I was out. No goodbyes. Some things were missing from the house. I had a letter about a year later. A little money inside. A token apology. Since then no word.'

He had to ask.

'Do you remember where the letter was sent from?'

'Keep on south, over the mountains and as far as you can go. This is where they were headed, I know. But Judy's mother is so restless in her spirit, I do not think you will find them.'

40.

The man was wretched. He had built his world on the sand of meaningful self-sacrifice. But this picture of his daughter being dragged along by an unstable mother from one unsuitable liaison to another, it made nonsense of everything.

He had acted instinctively that hellish night, in taking the blame and protecting others. Since then, the only way through had been to hold on to the rightfulness of what he had done, and why. He was no longer so sure. He had perverted the course of justice. Maybe he had done wrong, by everyone. It occurred to him for the first time that no-one would thank him for his actions. Neither Judy, later in life, nor her mother, pursued by unresolved guilt. Certainly not the dead man's father.

There hadn't been time to sit and discuss the pros and cons with someone sensible. He had been forced to act decisively, and he had done so in good faith. Or had he? Was it not the sweet notion of his heroism and his sacrifice which had seduced him? The little badge his mind had made for itself read 'noble martyr'. He should perhaps scrub that out and write 'vain fool' instead. He might make an enemy of himself with a little truthfulness.

The reward of their hard morning's climb was an extended downhill. The cyclist's greatest joy. But in the inverted world of despair, the man saw only its inconveniences. For the steepest sections he clung to the brakes to retain control until his wrists ached. On the serpentine corners there was the skid of loose gravel along the road edge, to which the bicycle was banished by the roadhogging engines of indulgence. He had to concentrate so hard on staying upright, he had no leisure to look about and enjoy the ease of his freewheel. And it was all over far too soon, without the extensions of real pleasure. His senses had been battered, rather than beguiled. His ears invaded by a roar of wind, his eyes tearful and fly-blown, his nose an unmentionable stream.
And yet. And yet the black of his disillusion, the grey of his self-recrimination, these were no match for the blue of a mediterranean sky. For the green and gold of high summer. For the russet curls of Argus and the pink of his hot, distended tongue. For the light brown of the girl's country skin, and the billowing white of her unbuttoned shirt.

Their journey levelled out over the plain. His spirits were reviving. The bicycle was such a true friend. He could rant and swear at it from the depths of his misery, and its response was to spin quietly the magical revolution of redress. He was redeemed by the very mobility of his altar.

The girl tracked his war of colours without fear. She remained close. Ever since the night they arrived and tried to find the forest, she was confident of the man's reserves. He had the beating of his interior foes, at least. She was less sure how he would fare against circumstance.

They hated to travel with their backs to the mountain. They stopped by a freshwater lake, filled to the brim each spring by the migration of ice and snow. A great triangular silhouette of rock pressed upon the surface of the water. Argus leapt straight in, without a break in his stride for deliberation. They watched his hound-paddle with loving smiles. His movement through the water was rather graceful, his muzzle a steady, snorting conning-tower.

They turned to gaze at where they had been. The man stood behind the girl, holding her close and resting his chin in her hair. They readjusted to the scale of distance. The whole was visible again, but not the detail. That was supplied by a mix of memory and imagination.

They picnicked on a bank of grass by the water's edge. The girl had bought bread from the mountain village baker, whilst the man peered through the windows of the primary school opposite, at the neat row of desks and the drawings on the wall. There was cheese from the goat lady, and tomatoes from her garden. There was fruit, and water from the mountain stream which cascaded past her farm. After food they felt the fatigue of the morning's excitement. They laid out in the sun until their limbs were irradiated of their ceaseless cranking revolutions. Argus splashed and panted in the shallow water, inviting them in.

At last, they threw off the rest of their clothes, and felt the shock of the water's recent altitude. They had to keep moving to keep breathing. The pleasure was not so much in doing, as in having done. Their flesh tingled with well-being, as they lay on the bank and felt frost turn to fire.

41.

They feared for the lorry if they tried to drive over the chain of mountains. The engine might overheat on the way up, the brakes on the way down the other side. Instead they headed for the narrow strip of land between the chain's flank and the sea.

They bobbed up and down along the ancient coast road, tracing the teeth of a wide bay's grin. There were little fishing ports busy with trade, and fortified villages bursting with visitors who came not with bucket and spade, but with paintbrush and camera. The water and the light swirled together into a dazzling flame, around which artists had danced for over a century.

They camped for the night near the border, and pushed on South early the following morning into a land that felt harsh and savage. They resumed their rhythm of parking up in a favoured spot to inhabit the middle of the day.

By chance they came across the line of an old railway, which had been transformed into a path for walkers and cyclists. They knew nothing of where it went, but it promised adventure free from the tyranny of engines. It was a risk, leaving the lorry unattended in a municipal car park. But they chose a shady corner, then removed their valuables into the cycle panniers along with some clothes and a little food.

They travelled along the bed of a former railway, which had connected the highlands to the sea. Their progress was always slightly uphill, but against such a smooth, easy gradient that the pedalling never felt too opposed. They tilted at the same chain of mountains, but this time from the other side.

The surrounding country was less fertile. More arid. An enemy to the water of the high snows, which would rather evaporate up, or percolate down, than irrigate its crumbling surface. The quiet revolution of the spokes went uninterrupted for so long that in the heat the mind began to step free from the body's exertion.

They stopped to find water for Argus and to replenish their bottles. It was the point of no return that day. If they carried on it would mean spending the night away from the lorry. He hesitated.

'Are you enjoying this?'

The girl was animated.

'The solitude is wonderful. We have a railway to ourselves. And the rhythm of steady cycling in a straight line, it's quite mesmerising. Something I've never experienced before.'

'It's a diversion, but let's make the most of it, and see where we end up.'

On again, and the countryside around them became steeper as they approached the foothills. The railway engineers had plotted a course to follow the contours, but in places there were extended bridges of rivetted black iron to cross, and short tunnels dug into the hillside. Without warning, they arrived at a longer tunnel. The darkness inside was intimidating, and complete.

The man pressed on a light switch mounted high up by the arch of the tunnel's opening. Nothing happened. He cursed.

'Usually there are lights all through these tunnels on timer switches. But some locals don't like to see the tourists. They would prefer to use the tracks for their own purposes, such as racing up and down in cars and on motorbikes. So they come and break the lights, as often as they are repaired.'

'I'm not going in there, in the pitch black. Have you got a torch, or a match even?'

'No. I didn't think of bringing one.'

'Then let's turn round, and go back. It's been fun to reach this far.'

The man made no move. He stood at the entrance, lost in thought. The girl grew restless.

'Come on. We might wait here for hours until someone else cycles along. And then they might be just as unprepared as we are.'

The man turned towards her, looking suddenly pleased with himself.

'What are you, in that tunnel, without light?'

'Lost. Frightened probably. Vulnerable. Bloody terrified in

fact. So let's get going. It's all downhill, so we might make it back before dark.'

'No, not that. Something more straightforward. In there, you're blind. You enter the blind man's world. Do you know what it feels like, to experience the world without sight? Not in childhood games, I mean for real. To have to go forwards, with no knowledge of what's in front, and no vision?'

'No. I don't, and I bet you don't either.'

'Exactly. This is not a problem, it's an opportunity. How does the blind man see?'

'With a stick.'

The man had propped his bicycle against the arch, and was walking back to where some bushes grew beside the track. He picked out two sturdy branches, a couple of metres long, and trimmed each one to make it light and manouvreable.

'You're left-handed, so you walk on the left with the bicycle in your right hand and this in the other, held out until it touches the tunnel wall. If you keep a steady contact with the wall, then you must walk in a straight line along the track bed. I'll do the same on the right.'

'And what about Argus?'

'He can look out for himself. Come on. We'll try it.'

They moved forward together. At first, there was still the light from the entrance behind them. But the tunnel began to curve to the right, and soon they were cut off from their world entirely. Argus followed on, using his nose to navigate. They could hear occasional growls of self-assurance.

'Don't speak. Let's be transported.'

The air became cold and humid. The scratching of their branches made little impression on the damp, thick silence. They looked forward, eager to see a spot of light ahead. Had they noticed the plaque above the tunnel entrance, they would have known it was several kilometres long. At a cautious walking pace, there were at least twenty minutes of another life to experience.

They observed the vow of silence. Speech was the only reassurance they might have had. Without it, the brain was unbraked, disembodied and left to spin too fast, too free. Terror. Panic. Claustrophobia. Monstrous imaginings. Each wave gave reason a ducking, and held it under until it could burst free.

There was a calm beyond. A state of cool repossession. And liberation. I can do this. I just fell apart, but now I'm back together again. Their pace quickened. The endorphins swirled and spread their elation.

It was a breakthrough. They ran the last section towards the day, their screams and barks curdling deep beneath the earth. Now they were blind in the light. They danced and hugged and wrestled with Argus. So playful and exhilarated. A new joy undiminished.

42.

The end of the line was a fortified medieval village, cradled by mountains. The old station building had been converted into a bar and restaurant, with half a dozen simple bedrooms above.

They went in. A lady came to the tiny reception desk, and offered them supper, bed and breakfast at a reasonable rate. They had little cash, but the girl said she would use her credit card. At the last minute it occurred to them that Argus might not be welcome inside. Without the vocabulary to ask, they opened the door and pointed to the hound, and to themselves. The lady was amused. No problem. More sign language to explain that they would need to buy food for him as well.

In the bar, they slaked their thirst with cool beer. The locals showed an interest in the eccentric foreigners who bicycled with their dog. Two hunting men were open in their admiration of Argus. They wanted to buy him. Since language was a problem, one telephoned his son and told him to come. He speaks good English, he told them proudly.

They went up to their room to shower and change before supper. By the time they came back down, a great hunger expanded inside them. But the son had arrived, and he was eager to show off his language skills. They had to sit through strange three-way conversations about hunting, sabotaged lighting and football.

The restaurant tables spilled out onto the old railway platform, which served well as a terrace. They sat beneath an awning of stars, with Argus at their feet gnawing his way into an exhausted ham. For them, there was salad, and tortilla and fish stew. Their looks were open ones of love.

'You're thinking this is the summit. It's all downhill from here.'

The man ignored the bait.

'I was just chewing on an old bone, like our friend down there. The different ways we travel, and why. It's the only politics I care for.'

He considered for a moment, before continuing.

'When you go somewhere in a car, how does it make you feel?'

'Comfortable. Protected. Mostly in control. Relaxed if the weather and the traffic conditions are in my favour. Stressed if they aren't. But I don't have a car, remember. And I gave the lorry to you.'

'Exactly. So travelling by car must have an underlying drawback, sufficient to put you off.'

'Yes. It's expensive.'

He grinned.

'You're playing with me, because you think you know where I'm headed. There's pleasure in driving, no doubt of that. But how is it that I have no respect for it? Because my conscience reckons the pleasure base. It comes from lazy self-indulgence. It makes me feel good for all the wrong reasons. There is no effort and no discipline in it. It feeds my desire for power, and my selfishness. As long as I'm alright, to hell with anyone else and the damage I may be doing. It encourages the unpleasantness in me.'

He paused, and watched the girl, waiting for a response. She took her time.

'I don't know that I've ever thought about it quite like that. I just can't afford it, neither the cost, nor the dependence on others for maintenance and repair.'

'Ah, so we're back to first positions. For you, it's independence. For me, it's merit. We might have driven up here today, and there would have been pleasure in the journey. We would still have had each other for company, and the sights to share along the way. But as I sit here now, I feel more than mere pleasure. I feel elation. The exercise has given me a sense of physical well-being. And the discipline of bicycling has unlocked the feelgood of achievement. Had I walked, it might be the same. But as long as I indulge myself with an engine, I destroy the merit. And the sense of adventure.'

'I don't think you'll get very far in politics with a message like that. Down with self-indulgence. What a slogan that would make.' They sat eating fruit, and reviewing their journey so far. Neither wanted the day to end. They set off to wander in the village, through narrow, cobbled streets beneath delicate balconies of wood and ironwork. Their walk was a parry with unspoken sadness. They both sensed that they had reached the summit, but there was no indication how long they got to stay there. Before the gravity of diminution pulled them back down.

43.

For three days the lorry served them well. They followed the sea. First south, then west until they approached the region fixed upon to continue the search. There was a narrow coastal strip which was intensively developed, and zoned according to wealth. A sandy walkway had been built behind the beach, with gaily painted railings, lampposts and flagpoles. It stretched for several miles across the bay, and here the population took their exercise, overlooking the sea. A host of walkers, joggers, roller bladers and cyclists negotiated their way up and down, set against a sea of sparkling reflections.

Behind the walkway were the millionaire mansions, with direct access to the beach through garden doors set in security fencing. Further inland was the main road and its strip of commercial development and high rise housing. After this the land began to lift toward the low mountains. Here were thousands of mid-price villas, in styles ranging from simple to splendid, and all with sea view terraces and swimming pools.

They stopped first in a car park behind a beach restaurant, and imagined lulled nights of lapping surf. But in the early evening a police car came to move them on. They fled toward high ground, following a road which snaked its way up through villa country to a mountain village. Here the tarmac ended, and they continued along a dirt track until they found uninhabited space.

The village had been built at a point where water gushed out of the limestone without ceasing. The villagers walked to the fountain, to gossip and fill their containers, and consider life. Once the lorry was parked out of the way, the three travellers strolled there too. There was no hostility or suspicion in the looks they received, just a friendly curiosity as they exchanged greetings.

The water was cool and delicious. It tasted of woodland, earth and rock. The man stumbled over his words of admiration, and the girl followed on with greater confidence. The villagers responded with pride, and pronounced it the best water to be found in that region.

A stone channel had been made to divert a stream into a series of descending open tanks. Before electricity came to the village, the women would come here to do their washing. They scrubbed and beat the clothes on slabs of gently grooved stone, and then rinsed them in the flowing tanks. No-one did so now, since every home could boast of an automatic washing machine.

The water still tumbled down the stairway of deep basins, giving the fountain area a cool calm enchantment, and a ghostly sense of working sisterhood. Technology was forever dividing them, breaking up their groups in the fields, at the fountain or in the square, and isolating them in their homes, or at their machines. The villagers seemed to sense their loss, and congregated still in the places they had once relied upon for their survival. Yet the gathering had a listless undertow, for the sense of purpose and necessity had been excised.

The journey to the sea from their campsite was fifteen kilometres of cycling heaven. They set off late morning, past the fountain, through the narrow white-washed streets and into groves of olive, citrus and avocado. Coming round a buttress of rock, they were greeted by a view of the town far below, then the sea, and beyond it the mountains of another continent. They glided on down in effortless freewheel, cosseted by sunshine and warm breezes. They used their brakes so as to savour the descent, and give Argus the chance to catch up.

They connected up with one end of the seafront walkway, and cycled its full length into the centre of the town. As long as they kept going forward, Argus was too busy running to get into mischief. But when they stopped to lean over the railings and marvel at the glistening silver blue of the sea, he soon became a danger to other traffic.

His ambassadorial charm and gentle curiosity were misconstrued by terrified mothers pushing their buggies, and elegant promenaders dressed for display. So they cycled on, past terraces of crisp linen set for lunch, and phalanxes of sunbeds beneath attendant solar banners.

The town centre arteries were furred with the cholesterol of high summer. They persevered long enough to get their bearings, but then gave up trying to wheel their bicycles through the throng and hold onto Argus at the same time. They escaped back to the beach with some food for a picnic. In a quiet corner they lay on the hot sand, eating and laughing. There was an attempt to bury Argus up to his neck, but he wouldn't stay still long enough.

The man changed into his trunks behind a towel. The girl already had her bikini on underneath. They ran at the surf, outpaced by Argus, who bit the waves and sneezed salt. The warmth of the water encouraged them to swim out to sea, from where they looked back at the layers of happy beach yellow, clean built white and stern mountain grey.

A lifeguard came down from his watching loft to tell them that dogs were not allowed on the beach in summer. He was pleasant enough about it. They packed up their things, and began to cycle back the way they had come.

The morning's freewheel was now a stinging, burning, endless test of will. The first bit was always the worst, at least for the man. Once mind and muscle had accepted the task, he loved to push against the opposing hand of gravity. It was all set out in front of you, and with only yourself to rely on. Rather that any day, than cycle on the flat against the wind, with its infuriating puffs of temperament, and its needling chill. On a climb, especially under a hot sun, he felt his whole skin perforate itself into a colander of sweat. He sensed a renewal.

The girl was less sure of the pleasure in it. But she relished her ability to make it to the top on her own, and not far behind. Argus bounded back and forth between them, urging on and weaving back together whatever split apart.

When they reached the fountain, all three plunged into the tanks of cool water, to rinse off the crust of sweat and sand. Throughout the evening they lingered by the lorry, eating, and laughing, and resting. The girl felt the physical well-being of it. Although she didn't say so, she felt the merit and the adventure too.

44.

     'I'll take Argus out for a good walk. See where this track leads. Then we can go down and do some research. I want to check the records at the Town Hall. Try some schools maybe. Get a copy of the local English language newspaper.'

     'And leave Argus in the lorry, on his own? Do you think that's wise? He might howl all day.'

     'It's worth a try. He's got his bed here, and he's bright enough to know that he's not being abandoned forever.'

Later they breakfasted on fruit and fresh bread which the girl had bought in the village market. And there was a large bone too, which she had charmed out of the butcher. Argus took it to his lair underneath the bed platform. They gently closed the folding door, and moved off down the track out of sight. After several minutes there was still no reaction from inside the lorry.

     'We'll only be gone a few hours, the time to do a search in town, and have a swim in the sea. He'll be fine.'

There was a group of local youths hanging out at the fountain. They exchanged a greeting and cycled on through the village towards the long descent. They were not concerned at the presence of the youths.

Much of the commercial centre of the town had been renewed and rebuilt during the last twenty years, especially either side of the main road. There were smart banks, with facades of white marble, fashionable shops set in glass and tall department stores. In the centre was a park, whose paving stones were hosed down early each morning. Men read the paper by day on its cool, shady benches, or played chess around stone tables.

Behind this district was the old quarter, quite untouched by the new development. Here they found the town hall, which dominated an elegant cobbled square of restaurants and tourist cafés. They asked to see the register of electors, and searched through its names in vain. They compiled a list of likely schools and social venues. And they circulated through the town's streets, their eyes and ears alert to home signals.

It was decided that for lunch they might treat themselves to a snack at a beach restaurant. Beneath the shade of a garish parasol, they ate tuna salad and felt as light-headed as parents out without the children. Such ambivalence, to know a relief from responsibility and yet miss its confinement.

They walked to a school which was patronised by many English speaking parents, or so they were told. Their visit was timed to coincide with the pupils' return from the midday siesta. They sat on a wall opposite the school gates and watched and waited for the children to return to their classrooms. In vain, since the holidays had already begun.

The man grew depressed, whenever he was faced with the hopelessness of his quest. They returned to the beach, where they immersed themselves in the warm, blue water to brine away the sadness and despair.

Back up the serpentines of the mountain road, and this time their legs felt heavy without the unshakable enthusiasm which Argus brought to their lives. He was a distraction from the tedium of certain moments, a jester to their court, a cheerleader to their daily jousting. It was only now, without him for the first time, that they could truly know how much they fed on his endless happiness. He revelled in so much that they frittered away, with their doodles of circular reasoning. He was the antidote to their angst, the talisman to ward off their fear.

The thought of the coming reunion gave new force to their limbs, carrying them up the last of the climb to the village. The girl paused at the fountain to quench her thirst.

'Stay there and cool off. I'll go and fetch Argus. He'll be glad of a splash.'

The man cycled on along the track towards their campsite, smiling at the memory of their shared bath the day before. Each one immersed in a tank of mountain water. His smile was ripped from his face when he rounded the last bend. He could see there was something very wrong.

45.

The youths had watched them cycle away that morning. These strangers, where did they come from along the track? There were no houses, no hotels in that direction. It led to woodland, and olive groves. After that, only up into the mountain.

They spent the mornings hanging around the village, in the hope that something interesting would turn up. There wasn't much else to do. After the siesta, they fired up raucous motorbikes and went down to the beach or into town, a swarm of two-stroke bees. But the mornings were empty. They dragged so.

The pack had its leader. He was tall and athletic, which had given him an early confidence. His parents owned the village bar and restaurant. They had worked hard, and could afford to spoil their only son. The other youths looked up to him, and envied his easy success, both at school and with the girls.

The leader knew of a pretender to his throne, of one who resented rather than admired his prowess. Albeit secretly. He recognised the fleeting looks of envy, even if he didn't understand them. They brought a tension to the affairs of the pack, which few identified but all enjoyed. Through competition came power.

Their leader led them in search of entertainment that morning. Along the track where the foreigners had been, to see what might be there. They wandered for a bit, but found nothing unusual. Heat began to chase away the upland cool. They grew languid and quarrelsome. There were voices of protest, urging a return to the village. But the leader persisted, to test his command. Once past the shoulder of rock they saw the lorry.

There was a hush of excitement, and fear. They approached the strange vehicle and surrounded it, trying to see in the windows. The front windscreen was curtained off to keep out the hot sun. The youngest boy got on the leader's shoulders to look through the back window. He said he could see a bed, some clothes, a little kitchen area with food, some personal stuff, but nobody inside.

The leader went round to the side entrance. He pulled at the folding door, to see if it was locked from the other side, but it opened up to his touch. He was wrongfooted by that. He had expected it to be locked. Then he might have let down the tyres, or stolen the windscreen wipers so that honour was satisfied, and they could all scarper. Now he must go in, or else lose face. He had no idea what to do once inside, but it didn't look good to hesitate too long, so he stepped up into the lorry.

As he did so, a movement to the right caught his attention. He had time so see a large dog launch itself from under the bed with a big bone in its mouth. The bone saved him. It took a second for the dog to realise that it could neither bark nor bite as things were. It must abandon the bone first. In that second the boy retreated backwards down the step and slammed shut the door. There were furious howls of protest from within.

The leader's heart raced with fear. He hated dogs. But he considered he had come out of it quite well. He hadn't fallen over backwards, or forgotten to shut the dog in. There was no discredit in his withdrawal. He strove for dignity as he moved away from the door.

Alas, the pretender saw the leader's fear. His heart raced with joy. Here was an opportunity to undermine the other's authority. He taunted the leader, urging him to go back in. Surely he wasn't afraid of a barking dog. The others were excited by the challenge. It hadn't happened so openly before. The leader felt their looks and their anticipation. His fear sunk from his heart to his stomach, and made him want to retch. He couldn't go back in, but he saw no way of excusing himself.

Diversion was his instinctive defense. If you're so brave, why don't you go in there yourself? But he played into his rival's hands. The pretender had no fear of Argus. He had been brought up with his father's hunting dogs. Now he had the attention he so craved. The spotlight was his for the taking, and he moved into it with a display of casual command. From one of the gang he demanded a jacket, which he wrapped around his left forearm. From another a belt, with which to strap the jacket in place. He had seen the police train their Alsatians this way.

Someone else pulled open the door, and he flung himself up the step, holding his left arm out in front for protection. He didn't know quite what to expect. He was too full of adrenalin to care. Argus came at him, and snapped onto the arm that was thrust in his way. They pushed and pulled. Stalemate. Then the boy had an idea. He would grab something to hit the dog with, and knock it unconscious. He looked behind towards the kitchenette, for a saucepan or a plate. At that moment Argus pushed forward, catching the boy off balance and launching him backwards against the counter. Letting go the arm, he bit again. This time between the boy's legs.

The pain was unbearable. The others outside heard his scream, and felt the terror of misadventure. Argus had the boy pinned back against the kitchenette, with his jaw locked onto the invader's genitals. The boy became light-headed, and feared losing consciousness. Nobody came to his rescue. He reached around with his right hand and searched the worktop for anything to use as a weapon. His hand closed on a bread knife. He jammed it down into the side of Argus' rib cage.

The jaw released him. He stumbled out into the group. He must not yield his advantage. Do not show fear or injury. The dog bit me so I stabbed it, he said as calmly as his agony would allow. Let's get out of here. His first words as leader. He blocked out the pain with new pleasure.

Argus lay on his side. His breathing was irregular. The knife had punctured a lung. His only thought was to find the man. He was already weak, and bleeding profusely. When he tried to stand up, he couldn't. He scrabbled his way to the door, and fell down the step out into the midday heat. The knife caught on the door on the way down, and opened up the wound. He was very thirsty. He tried to lick where the blood flowed out. He must find the man. Find the girl. Protect them. Yet he could feel his life force seeping away into the earth.

46.

The man pulled out the knife and flung it into the bushes. He rolled Argus' body in a rug and laid him in his lair under the bed. He couldn't think what else to do.

Then he started to walk back to the girl. Shock gave way to misery. He couldn't stop the tears. When she saw his face, she understood. Only one thing could overwhelm him so.
　　'Argus must have been trying to defend the lorry. Someone stabbed him. I think he bled to death.'
They clung together. Nothing would console. They cried by the fountain and reached deep into each other's sadness.

He led her back to the lorry. They lay side by side on the bed above Argus' body, and became numb with despair. When night came, they were still there. They felt no hunger even though they hadn't eaten since the restaurant. How delicate is life's motherhood. Just a little slip, and then her protective embrace is gone. Maybe for good.

The girl lay on her back, looking at the stars through the skylight window. She couldn't sleep whilst her mind churned so with guilt. She might have insisted that they didn't leave Argus, when she had known from the start that it wasn't a good idea. Too late for that. Another guilt was greater. She would go home now, and that meant leaving the man when he needed her most. She turned on her side to look at him.

'I can't go on with your search. Not now. I need to find a way back to England. Come with me, to the farm. I know we can make a life there worth living.'

He had been waiting for this. He realised that nothing could be as before. The tears threatened to overwhelm him once more.

'And what would I say to my daughter, if ever I chanced to meet her one day? That I came looking for her once, but somebody killed my dog so I turned back? You cannot imagine how much I yearn for a life there at Charrafin with you. But every day without Judy is a day of unspoken pain. If I give up now, I will be hollow and of no use to you. Yet if I continue, I will be destroyed. I know that. The possibility of finding her is so small, and even if I do it may turn out horribly unpleasant for everyone. Please tell me I'm wrong. Tell me I don't have to go on.'

His look was so charged with sadness, so full of entreaty. She couldn't stay with it. She turned away, in silence. There was nothing to say.

A few birds began to sing very early, with the first light of dawn. The man got up and started the lorry's engine. He drove it into a clearing away from trees and vegetation. He packed a few essentials into his panniers, and advised the girl to do the same. With a hammer and chisel he hacked off the engine's serial number and the lorry's registration plates and then destroyed them. He took a bucket and crawled underneath on his back to where the fuel tank was bolted to the chassis. He cut through the hoseline and filled the bucket with petrol, allowing the rest to drain away into the earth. He removed the gas bottle, then splashed petrol over the bed and the shelving and the kitchenette, making a trail backwards along the ground until he was a safe distance away.

'It's still yours really. You set it alight.'

She hesitated. But somehow it was right. She threw down a lighted match and they watched the fire race forwards to ignite the lorry. Flames leapt high out of the open skylights. The wooden frame and bookshelves burnt with an intense heat. Soon there was nothing to support the outer skin of aluminium which melted and collapsed inwards.

The fire began to die back. Only the tyres were still burning strongly. They said goodbye to a friend. They would think of him and miss him always. Nothing could take his place. The man was aware too that Argus had been a presence in his life beyond friendship. They had come together in the quarry, they had fought together out of it, where once the man had struggled side by side with his brother against the forces of the fearful unknown. Argus had saved his life. He had been the spirit of his brother reincarnated, to see him through adversity and on towards rebirth. Henceforth he would have to manage on his own.

They turned their backs, and cycled down the track. They stopped at the fountain for a final blessing, and to fill their water bottles. The village was still quiet. The houses were shuttered and blind. They began the descent to the sea. A fire engine screamed past them, coming up from the town. Somebody must have noticed the smoke.

47.

They headed west again, following the old coast road. The terrain was mostly flat, easy cycling. There was no-one to distract them, or draw them into their surroundings. No-one to wait for, or hurry to catch up. No link with outer life. Their loss isolated them entirely.

They pedalled hard and fast, blinkered by grief. There was solace in the exhilaration of their speed. Distraction in the pain they began to feel in their legs and their lungs. The body's suffering was a relief.

By early evening they had reached a promontory of massive rock. There was a queue of pedestrians and cars at the border crossing. They stood in line to show their passports, then walked across the airport runway into the little town scrunched at the foot of the Rock. It felt like a world of childhood imagining. In other circumstances the change of scale and culture might have been remarkable. On this day, their dislocation was continuous and complete.

The girl went into a travel agent to buy a ticket home. The man stayed outside with the bicycles. She emerged a while later having booked a seat on a flight later that evening. It's better this way, she said.

They went to a hardware shop and bought a large sheet of bubble wrap and some sticky tape. The man took her bicycle to pieces. The wheels, the pedals, the handlebars and the seat, they all came off and were wrapped together in a parcel no bigger than the bike's frame. From several layers of tape he fashioned a carrying handle so that it would be easy to move around when she arrived the other end.

At the check-in they waited in a long line of returning holidaymakers. Pink and peeling mostly. The girl wanted to go through to the departure hall straightaway.

'Let's get it over with. I'll sit and wait on my own. You need to find somewhere to stay.'

They clung to each other again, but somehow in their hearts the parting had already been made. There was no recrimination. Each knew the other had little choice. They both believed that a life together was worth striving for. And yet neither of them, in their sadness, could see it happening.

The girl turned and went through passport control. She didn't look back. She couldn't look back. The man remained standing still in the terminal lounge and felt the last of his hope go with her. He had no more chance of finding his daughter than he had of finding his God.

He crossed back to the mainland and headed for the port. He calculated that he had at least enough money for the short crossing to another continent. After that he didn't know or care.

By the time he arrived it was too late to catch the last ferry. He looked about for somewhere to spend the night. There was a stone seat set in the harbour wall. He lay back, with his head resting on his panniers, and the bicycle cable-tied to his waist, as once before he had done on a railway platform. He saw himself as he was then, and longed for the naivety of such hope.

His body was tired, his mind weak with the exhaustion of despair. Yet sleep, the coy restorer, wouldn't come. The wall still held the sun's heat, which only reminded him of his solitude. He had grown accustomed to the mystery of shared warmth, after the sterile years of imprisonment. Now he must do without again. He must survive on the resources he might generate for himself. Alone. This was a true understanding of existence. Anything else was but a delusion for the fearful.

Sometime later in the night he fell asleep. He dreamed of a desert, of an endless expanse of furrowed sand which he was trying to cross on a bicycle. But the wheels were sinking down and taking him with them. He wouldn't let go. He woke and jumped to his feet. There was a figure standing by him, tugging on the bicycle handlebars. He bellowed with the full force of his lungs. It was an ancient cry, an unthinking scream of pain and rage. The figure shrunk back and ran off.

He settled down again, but now adrenalin kept him awake. He thought of the girl, landed and probably making her way home by bus or train. Charrafin. The name which had inspired her tears. He might find his own place beyond the plough, in a country made up of sand. In a land where things had rubbed together without water for so long that only their essential dust remained.

He slept as dawn spread over the sea. Its light reassured him. He heard voices. Slowly their murmurings and laughter coaxed him out into the daylight. When he opened his eyes there was a ripple of applause. He could see faces turned towards him, talking and smiling. There was a long file of people on the pavement next to him. Housewives with shopping bags, men in work clothes and a few young children. He couldn't make it out. What were they doing there? Then he saw the coach swinging out from the junction and coming to a practised halt at the bus stop. The audience excused themselves, with more smiles and a few goodbyes. They were summoned by all manner of happiness, and misery. He sat up as the coach pulled away, and held up a hand in greeting. It was the most fleeting friendship of his life, and yet one of the most moving. Rather than wake him, they had watched him sleep. They had preferred to stand rather than disturb him. They had been as parents might have been to a young child. Watchful, patient, protective. And yet they knew nothing of the stranger, the foreigner asleep on their seat.

48.

To cross the narrow stretch of water and land on another continent felt like a renewal of sorts. It made room for other possibilities. He felt lighter somehow.

When he cycled into the town, he realised why. He no longer had the lorry to cocoon himself from his surroundings. The sights and sounds and smells were no longer filtered through glass and tin. They assaulted him directly. He felt their energy, and his exposure to their demands. He had lost the lazy convenience of his motorised sofabed. There was little money left to buy respite. That felt good, that held back the sense of futility. He was no longer superfluous in his own life.

He went to the train station to find out about timetables and fares. His vision of a land that was featureless and dry had begun to take hold. If he cycled he would need at least a week to reach the south. Whereas if he took the train as far as the railway went, he might go from there by bicycle, up over the last great mountain range, and within days he would know the comfort of expanded emptiness.

He should be able to afford a second class seat on the overnight train, if there was something left to sell. His bowie-knife was the obvious choice. Everything else, except his bivi-bag and a change of clothes, had been abandoned in the lorry. His passport he should save for an emergency. In the medina he tried several traders but no-one would offer him a fair price. It was a good knife. He knew its value, and so did they but he was unwilling to begin haggling until he had done the rounds.

He decided to try the tourist cafés and restaurants in the new town. The idea that he should beg humbly from his own kind appealed to him. He was an unhappy vision. His face was dirty from travelling and part covered in stubble. His clothes tattered and stained. The bicycle he pushed along at his side looked like the sort of thing somebody else might have thrown away, as indeed somebody had. His eyes had the stare of one who no longer clings to life, but rather anticipates an end.

He moved from table to table, offering his knife for sale in a mixture of English and French. It made the diners uncomfortable, to see someone from their own world demean himself that way. They could not wave him away, as they might have done with another beggar. Neither did they want to engage with his sadness. He was offered food by one woman. Half her pizza which had failed to stimulate an appetite. He ate leaning against his bicycle at the side of the street and ignored a waiter who tried to move him on.

He wandered again through the narrow streets of the medina. One advantage of looking so abandoned was that everyone avoided him, including the nagging children and persistent traders who would normally have preyed upon a tourist. He haggled with one stallholder for a while, but eventually accepted less than the knife was worth. At least he had enough now to journey south on the train, and leapfrog over the ploughland.

The disintegration had been so rapid. There was still a part of him which observed things from another life and was amazed. One minute he was locked into a triangle of strength with Argus and the girl. Self-contained and optimistic. The next, it seemed as if the sides of the triangle had collapsed into a single line of least resistance. Leading to emptiness. Nothingness. To the end of a hopeless search. That, at least, would be a relief. To find a place beyond searching, where he might cast aside his senseless burden.

At the station he hung around, watching the general frenzy of travel and waiting for the night train. He saw his bicycle loaded into the freight wagon, along with all manner of mopeds and dilapidated two-wheelers. It did not look out of place, he was pleased to see. He did not want to be remarkable. He wanted to pass unnoticed on his journey.

49.

He was wedged into the corner of a carriage. The train rattled its way south through the night. He slept in brief snatches, with one pannier clasped on his lap and the other as a pillow. The relative cool of the evening made the stuffy compartment almost bearable.

He could see little of the scenery projected through dusty glass beneath a glossy sky. For some of the journey he was aware of the Atlantic creased alongside the track. The further he went towards the Equator, the more he felt dwarfed by both land and sea. Natural forces still held dominion here over human desire.

They arrived at the terminus mid-morning. He was hungry and thirsty, but he chose to ignore the demands of his body. At the doors to the freight wagon he waited while the two-wheelers and packages were handed down to the clamourous tangle of arms and heads on the platform. Now reunited with his bicycle, he pushed through the bustle towards the front of the station.

The buffers at the end of the track held his attention. He stood by the two great mushrooms of steel projecting from the concrete quay and recognised the spot for what it was. A line of demarcation. The iron horse pulled a certain train of industry and endeavour along with it. Here was where it ended. After this point, the returns no longer justified the investment. The curve of the track and the plough became alike. Henceforth uneconomic. This was the land he sought. His Charrafin.

He cycled through the streets of the new town, admiring the sweep of a boulevard or the detail of a minaret. Where the traffic was heavy, he preferred to walk alongside the bicycle, so as to drink in the dewy freshness of it all. He found his way to the medina, and then to a vast, open trading area surrounded by hotels, roads and restaurants.

This market square was unashamedly theatrical, thronged with every type of player from the simply authentic to the elaborately civilised. He wandered amongst the jugglers, acrobats, storytellers, scribes,snake charmers and parties of excited tourists. The play had taken on an energy of its own, such that everyone there was both actor and spectator alike. It was the largest informal theatre in the world, with one endless well-rehearsed performance. A few small coins bought him a bowl of chick-peas, ladled from a great boiling vat, and a round loaf of bread. He sat on the ground with his bicycle in order to eat and was absorbed by the spectacle all around him.

The backdrop to the south was a towering mountain range, holding back the endless desert beyond. He studied its outline with a certain fear. Tomorrow he would set out to pedal himself up and over to the other side. He calculated that it would take a day's cycling to reach the base of the mountains. Another day to ascend to the high pass, if his stamina held out. He had never before attempted an unbroken climb of over two thousand metres. His ancient bicycle with its few gears and inefficient brakes was not the vehicle of choice. Yet he welcomed the obstacle in his path, and the awe the mountains inspired in him. They would be a test of his will. A proof of his desire to see beyond.

By evening, the square expanded into an open-air restaurant and concert platform. Groups of musicians played to restless circles of audience. They drifted from one performance to another. Lines of cooks set up their kitchens beneath strings of electric lights, surrounded by trestle tables and narrow benches.

The man couldn't afford to pay for a bed, even in the cheapest hotel. He wandered and watched and listened through the night, as the waves of early evening tourists gave way to the prowls of native adventurers. The air remained warm and laden with meat and spice. In the early hours of the morning, the play petered out. The audience drifted away, and the last of the stallholders packed up their wares and their kitchens into vans or onto handcarts. For a while, the great market square was quiet.

The interval was short. The man watched the first light of dawn colour in the sky and catch the mountain tops. The rubbish lorries and street cleaners began to arrive, to prepare the stage for another display. He gathered up some fruit which had been discarded, along with a little stale bread, and stowed these provisions in one of his panniers. He sat astride his bicycle and was fascinated to see the first activities of a new day. It began all over again. It was relentless.

He set off on his journey south towards the mountains. As he crossed the square, he performed his own brief cycle-on part, before turning his back on the stage.

50.

He passed through groves of orange and lemon, which had been planted on the last of the fertile plain. There was little traffic on the road to cover him in its dust. The air was still only warm from the night, but he felt the early sun renewing its heat.

He climbed his way into hilly country. The farming was now restricted to the terraces surrounding any settlement. In between, the land was covered in woodland scrub. He stopped once at a roadside shop to buy bottled water. It made his progress easier if he did not try to carry all the water he needed to drink in order to avoid dehydration. The sweat ran down the inside of his legs, down his back and off his forehead to sting his eyes.

The further he cycled beyond the buffers, the more interest he aroused. Children shouted out to him, or raced alongside asking his name and where he was from. Some threw stones at him. It made no difference. He ignored the hostility and smiled at the interest. He knew better than to stop.

When the sun's power became unbearable, it drove him off the road into the shade of some almond trees. He ate his scraps of food scavenged from the square, and rested with his back against a tree trunk and his eyes fixed upon the mountains ahead. He measured the coming leap.

By late afternoon he was impatient to be on the move again, even though the air beyond the shade was still a furnace. He wrapped his head in a scarf of cotton, which trailed down over the back of his neck. With the buttons undone, his shirt flapped around the sides to cool his chest. He was thankful that his progress south over the last week had been slow enough to enable his body to acclimatise. So far he had prospered in the heat.

He stopped again to buy water. He checked the plastic seals on the caps to be sure that he didn't drink from used bottles which had been refilled. It was necessary to keep the last of his change to buy water. Otherwise he would not be able to maintain his health, for the challenge ahead.

By nightfall he reached the base of the mountains. There was a village set back from the road, clinging to the early slopes. Its walls and buildings were made of rammed earth and baked clay. He skirted round and found a place to spend the night, up high on the terraces behind the houses. He was tired and hungry. He rolled himself inside his bivi-bag as a protection against the insects and the cool upland air which tumbled down the mountainside. He slept the sleep of the willingly exhausted. The peak way above pulled his dreams high into flight.

He bought bread, fruit and water in the village the next morning. A round, flat loaf of bread fresh from the oven, which he ate with large segments of orange. He had three bottles of water with which to ration his climb to the pass. The shopkeeper told him that there was nowhere else to buy provisions until he reached the plain the other side. It made little difference. He had spent the last of his money.

51.

He described a serpentine. For every metre of ascent, there were many more of sideways prevarication. He was glad of the road's meanderings. It gave him a chance to look around and see the change in his surroundings as he moved higher. He liked the sensation of facing one way, then another. He could glance back down, and appreciate his progress from the dwindling scale of his starting point.

Besides, it was the best way to take on mountain gravity. Never with a straight assault, but rather with the hypnotic pendulum swings of the switchback approach. This confused gravity, and bamboozled away her self-belief.

He took advantage of the early morning coolness. His target was to cycle non-stop for at least four hours. There was no let-up. The road's zig-zags were a steady climb. No flat or downhill to recuperate. His energy went through many transformations. At first it fizzed with excitement, and he had to prevent himself from setting off too fast. Then he felt flat. His legs were dead and he was afraid he had nothing in him left to give. At last, he found a rhythm. The energy began to feed through steadily as his confidence returned. His body was at optimum temperature in the sober early sun.

There was little other traffic. He had chosen this route for that reason. The main highway across the mountains was twenty miles to the east, and enjoyed far better maintenance. The buses and lorries chose the safer, wider carriageway through the other pass. This way was reserved for occasional local journeys. It made all the difference to his cycling. He needed to fill his lungs so deeply with the thin air, in order to keep pedalling against the gradient. It would have been torture to rely for sustenance upon the clouds of black poisonous fumes which hung about the main road's toiling engines.

For a while he kept pace with the rising sun. As fast as it burnt into the haze of the lower slopes, he moved up towards the cool of altitude. His sweat was steady, not profuse. He limited his liquid intake accordingly. He could feel the beginning of a soreness between his legs. He cursed himself for not having found water with which to wash the night before.

After three hours climbing his body wilted. The heat had risen to overtake him. His legs wobbled. He could no longer force round the crank whilst seated, and he had become too sore to want to sit. He stood up on the pedals, and used his weight rather than his evaporated strength to keep the wheels turning. The bicycle rocked from side to side as he transferred the weight across and back. The motion increased the mobility in his lower spine.

He could only stand up for so long. However hard he breathed through clenched teeth, he knew he would have to stop soon. He told himself to carry on until the next available shade. The tree line was below him. He was surrounded by arid scrub. When he saw the wall of a tumbledown shelter, he left the road and collapsed into the narrow strip of shade. The stones smelt of goat. He drank hard from his last bottle and lay back to sleep.

When he set off again sometime later, he argued with fear. There was no way of knowing how far it was to the pass. He was forced to wonder whether he would make it there before dark, assuming he made it that far at all. There was nothing to distract him, nothing to relieve his ordeal. It would have been so much better with Argus, and the girl.

At dusk, he was still climbing. He heard the grind of a lorry on the road below. It did not feel safe to be all alone and without lights in such a remote spot. He pulled off the tarmac and crouched low amongst the scrub. The lorry came past. It set down such a trail of sooty black from the exhaust that it might have been sent forth to issue the night. A dozen figures stood silent and still in the open body. Not even their eyes were visible inside the deep hoods of their burnous.

The serpentines faded out. He had reached a plateau. He allowed himself to believe he was nearly there. But the road continued on through barren high country, with no end in sight. The disappointment undermined him. He was cold, hungry, sore and very tired. It was becoming dangerous to continue without light. He could not see the potholes to avoid them.

It came to him suddenly that he was no longer pedalling. The bicycle was coasting forwards by itself. For the first time that day. The feeling was strange, but exhilarating. He had made it. He encountered the first zigzag of descent. There beside the road was a car park hewn into the rock, with a small concrete building at one end. There was a terrace, with tables and chairs set out, and light from several windows. A café restaurant. He felt such relief.

Inside, a fire was burning in the corner chimney-piece. A few customers sat at tables gathered round it. He joined them, and tried to feel warm again. A man came from behind the bar to take his order. There was some discussion in broken French, followed by a short haggle. He exchanged his spare set of clothes for hot, sweet tea and a plate of almond biscuits. He had the use of a floor to sleep on for the night.

52.

He was up before the sun. He sat on the terrace wrapped in his bivi-bag and shivered not with cold but with excitement. From his watching loft over two thousand metres above the plain he saw a dark world reveal itself. The view south was endless. In the foreground, foothills and an ancient walled town. In the middle distance bare, barren ridges interspersed with narrow, fertile strips of palm-grove. Beyond that, nothing but sand.

A young girl came out onto the terrace. She could have been no older than ten, or eleven. One of the proprietor's family, he guessed. She looked at him with shy fascination. He smiled at her with the wonder of his morning's revelation. She returned in a few minutes with tea and more almond biscuits. He protested that he could not pay. She waved away his words and invited him to drink.

So many times he had sat down to tea and biscuits. Never like this. Never again like before. He knew that if he smelt almond, or the hot, sweet vapours of mint tea, he would be here once more. Floating above the world. Beyond reach. Beyond desire.

He would have stayed. With a little money to his name, he would have sat and stared day after day into cool, cloudless space. He would have watched the local traffic grind up,up and eventually on past. The soaring of the vultures, the rising and the setting of the sun. These would have been enough. The suspension of that lay-by high above life was perfect for his abstention. But he could accept no more kindness and hospitality without the means to pay. He dragged himself back to the bicycle and contemplated the descent.
They waved him off, standing on the terrace. The owner, the young girl and one of the guests from the night before. They wished him God's speed and a safe journey. The man stood on the pedals as he freewheeled down and raised a hand to acknowledge their farewells. He remained standing all the way to the plain below. He felt too sore to sit. His brake blocks were so worn, he could hear their metal grind

against the wheel rims. He kept the brakes squeezed on, for he knew that if once he allowed the bicycle to gain speed, he would not be able to control it again. It suited him to descend slowly, reluctantly, screechingly back to earth.

He fell once, as he skidded in the loose gravel of a hairpin bend. His hands, elbows and knees were left bleeding and embedded with grit. He had no water to spare for washing the cuts.

His spirits descended alongside him. The traffic, the human endeavour and the industry of the plain – they all repulsed him. He remembered his first day of freedom, and how he had embraced them then. Diminution was inexorable. He no longer cared for its gravity.

He pushed his bicycle through the huge gateway set in the wall of the town. In the medina he found someone willing to exchange his panniers for a few notes. They had rattled an empty reminder on the descent to annoy him. With the money he bought bread and bottled water. He tied his bivi-bag onto the frame and hid his passport in his pocket. The less he had to lose, the better it felt.

He headed south, through groves of palm. There were little villages of dried earth built around a well, or beside a water course. The barefoot children treated him savagely. He had the haunted look of an outsider. The wild dogs were worse. They chased him, sometimes in packs. He conserved what little energy he had for sprinting his escape, and cycled slowly between settlements.

To rest for the night he climbed into a tree, and pulled his bicycle up after him. It was the only way to escape the dogs, some of which appeared rabid. He used the frame and wheels to wedge himself in, and prevent a fall in his sleep. He felt very weak. His last proper meal had been days before,on a different continent and in a different lifetime so it seemed. Only the clean drinking water had kept him going this far. He had finished the last of it, with nothing left but his bicycle to sell.

The following day he thought obsessively of his thirst. He was nearing the end of the palm groves. The land around him was given over mostly to sand, with little shade. The heat from midday was overwhelming. He came across a well which was unattended, and lingered there. He had resolved never to drink from such a source, but his resolve was no match for his thirst. He winched up a bucketful of blackish water and drank.

The bright sun and the dust impaired his vision. He saw incandescent stars and strange shapes as he cycled. He fell again, thrown from his bicycle when the front wheel hit an unseen rock. He lay where he fell, in the dirt beside the road, to rest.

That inscription. VERITAS ODIUM PARIT. He understood it now. How the truth does hurt, like a bright light shone suddenly upon a flinching world of deception. Feelgood commands the brain. Feelgood is the motivator, scuttling out of the glare of truth into the shadows of ambiguity. And feelgood may be either counterfeit or real. The brain is pleased to approve both currencies. The one is an easy forgery, concocted in a basement of lazy delusion. The other a rare alchemy, a blend of instinct, faith and understanding.

Since regaining his freedom, the man had grown to prefer the discipline of honesty. Once he had done the wrong thing, for the wrong reason. It had landed him in prison. It had lost him his daughter. Never try to pass off vanity and egoism as noble sacrifice. But to live with truth he had to be strong, or at least have nothing left to lose. Suffering had brought him strength, and banished his fear.
He saw again the cycle ride he had taken with the girl and Argus up on the Moor. That was the beginning of truth. He had plunged his head into the stream, and felt naked, loving and alive. It had felt good to see straight on, instead of from an angle. The day was fixed in his memory as one of perfect happiness.

Face down in the sand, exhausted, bloody and feverish, he connected again with that happiness. It chased through him like a joyful spirit.

He felt the touch of the girl's fingers moving over his scalp and through his hair. He had known love. Love without reservation. He had been loved. That was enough. The dehydration and the heat overcame him. He lost consciousness.

53.

The kasbah was beautiful. Its high walls of rammed earth and straw enclosed a fertile oasis of over two acres. There was a gatehouse set in the south wall by the road, whilst the main building sprawled along the northern boundary overlooking the garden. A well in one corner pumped up water cool and compressed from the mountains. It spilled into channels of glazed clay and swirled throughout the enclosure. There were raised beds of vegetables, citrus fruits, avocado trees, tall palms, and olives, all laid out in a formal grid.

The village women carried his body to the gatehouse. They knew the kasbah as a place where foreigners stayed. They had found him lying unconscious by the road, as they returned to the village towards evening. They spent much of each day scouring the country in groups, singing, laughing and collecting firewood to fuel their ovens. They made a simple stretcher, using some of the branches they had gathered as well as material from their robes. They took turns to carry the weight of the man, three each side. They sang for the pleasure of saving him.

There was no way to identify the stranger. His bicycle had been stolen earlier, along with the passport from his pocket. Only the soiled clothes he lay in were left to him.

He was taken to the bathhouse. They washed away his journey with hot water and steam. He lay in an upstairs bedroom beneath a mosquito net. The walls were white-washed and unadorned. There was a window onto the garden, with louvred shutters of indigo blue.

He lay in a fever and fought for life. He wasn't sure he wanted it, but he didn't consent to give it up. His bed linen was changed when he had drenched it with sweat. His forehead was cooled with a compress of herbs from the garden. They managed to make him drink.

The man relived his ordeal. The humiliation of the trial. The terror of imprisonment. The strain of self-defence. There were bodies stabbed with knives, houses on fire and lost children. Sometimes he heard the beat of the pump, pulling up water from the well. Then the music of the streams, racing down channels beneath his window. He imagined that Argus was still with him, sleeping beneath the bed. He called out for the girl, but she never came.

In his delirium his legs kept pedalling, kicking off the sheets and tangling up his net. He flew from monstrous dogs covered in rabid spume. His bed was surrounded by hooded figures hurling rocks.

On the fourth day the fever relented. He heard birds singing in the garden. The song of a blackbird. The drip of a tap. He slept for long periods of calm. He became aware of his surroundings. The pure simplicity of white, with a splash of blue. The soft contours of an earthen wall. The short beams of palm wood. He knew the sounds of the gardener at work, with his hoe and his wheelbarrow made of wood.

He did not value his life, but he was happy to have survived. On the fifth morning he woke to sense someone seated by his bed. There was a small, sure hand stroking his forehead and hair. He turned on the pillow and opened his eyes. The young face looking down he claimed as his own.